Holly's Heart

Second-Best
Friend

Beverly Lewis

BETHANYHOUSE
Minneapolis, Minnesota

Published by Bethany House Publishers
A Ministry of Bethany Fellowship International
11400 Hampshire Avenue South
Bloomington, Minnesota 55438
www.bethanyhouse.com

Printed in the United States of America by
Bethany Press International, Bloomington, Minnesota 55438

Library of Congress Cataloging-in-Publication Data

Lewis, Beverly, 1949–
    Second-best friend / by Beverly Lewis.
        p.   cm. — (Holly's heart ; 6)
Rewritten version of: Second-best friend. Grand Rapids, Mich. :
Zondervan, c1994.
Summary: Holly struggles with jealousy when her best friend invites an
Austrian exchange student to stay for six weeks.
    ISBN 0-7642-2505-7
    [1. Friendship—Fiction. 2. Christian life—Fiction. 3. Jealousy—
Fiction. 4. Stepfamilies—Fiction.] I. Title.
    PZ7.L58464   Sde   2002
    [Fic]—dc21

                                                      2002002801

Author's Note

Cheers to my cool kid consultants: Mindie, Shanna, Kirsten, Amy, Janie, and Julie. And thanks, as always, to my SCBWI writers' group; Barbara Birch; and my husband, Dave, for their insight into the manuscript.

Special thanks to Kristie Frutchey, who shared information on the American Field Service, an international exchange student program. Also, to Lynn Sanders and Linda Marsh, of Aaron Animal Clinic in Colorado Springs, Colorado, for answering my questions about sick cats.

To
Kirsten Brown,
who loves cats so much
she wanted to take Melissa-Kitty
home from Swiggum's farm.

And . . .
To the memory of Kitty Tom,
a cool Kansas cat who lived
his life spoiled rotten.

"*I'm sorry, Goofey,* but you have to stay in my room tonight," I said, bending down to stroke my cat's motley fur. "Our stepdad's off his allergy pills for the weekend."

Goofey looked up at me. A brown patch of fur colored the gray around one eye. "Me-e-o-ow." It was as if he were apologizing for making my stepdad so miserable.

"It'll be okay, baby," I whispered. Not having the heart to tell him Mom's plan, I softly closed the door. Spending the entire weekend—every weekend—from now till who knows when locked away in a room was not something you discuss with your beloved thirteen-year-old tabby. But it was Mom's only solution to Uncle Jack's reaction to his allergy pills. For now.

Hurrying downstairs, I thought about Uncle Jack, who was once married to my dad's sister—

now in heaven. No blood relation, of course. His allergy medicine was making him drowsy. And for an upbeat, fun-loving guy, that was bad news. Tonight, though, things would be back to normal.

"Party time!" Uncle Jack called, tossing a round pillow at me as I entered the downstairs family room.

"Hooray!" cheered seven-year-old Stephie.

"Let's watch a Meredith home video," Carrie, my nine-year-old sister, suggested, pulling out one of our family before Daddy divorced Mom.

"Forget that," I said, playfully tugging it away from her.

"Let's rent *Deep Space Invasion*," suggested Mark, my eight-year-old cousin-turned-step-brother.

Phil, ten, tossed a baseball cap into the air. "Cool! Let's gross everyone out."

"Yeah, and when we get scared, we'll crawl into bed with Mommy and Uncle Jack," Carrie said. She scooted across the floor on her stomach, making room for me in front of the TV.

"Think again," sixteen-year-old Stan said, sprawling on the floor next to me. It was still weird having four cousins turn into three step-brothers and one stepsister overnight. "How 'bout a John Wayne movie?" Stan suggested.

"Not tonight, pilgrims," Mom said, snuggling

up to Uncle Jack. I sneaked a glance at them as they kissed. Still enjoying the honeymoon stage, no doubt.

"So . . . what are we watching?" I asked.

A comical grin sparked mischief in Uncle Jack's eyes. "You'll love this one," he said, popping a DVD into the player.

Everyone cheered when the title came on the screen. But *102 Dalmatians* wasn't exactly the kind of movie I was hoping for. Especially with Goofey stuck upstairs in my room instead of here purring next to me as usual.

Halfway through the movie we had intermission. Carrie and Stephie raced upstairs to their bedroom while Mom and Stan went to the kitchen to make ice-cream floats.

Thanks to the movie, I missed Goofey more than ever. I trudged upstairs to my room. When I got there, the door was open!

I scurried around my room, searching the closet and under my canopy bed. "Here, kitty, kitty," I called frantically. Man, would I be in big trouble if Mom found out Goofey was on the loose in the house.

And poor Uncle Jack! He'd been off his medicine since this morning, hoping for a stupor-free weekend.

Dashing downstairs, I looked everywhere. The living room, under the dining room table, in the kitchen. Worried, I ran to the lower level. That's when I saw disaster waiting to happen.

Loaded down with a tray of root beer floats, Mom couldn't see that Goofey was right on her heels! As she made her turn to the round coffee table, my cat leaped onto the sectional.

I crouched behind the sofa as Mom placed the tray of sodas on the wood surface. Reaching up, I tried to grab Goofey before Mom or Uncle Jack noticed him. But he leaped away, out of my grasp.

Oblivious to Goofey, Uncle Jack munched on popcorn. Then, reaching for an icy glass of root beer, he took his first drink. Meanwhile, Goofey—whose slightly torn ear flopped, reminiscent of his tomcat fight days—padded straight across the top of the sectional.

Then it happened! Goofey did the unthinkable. He curled himself around Uncle Jack's neck.

My stepdad jumped up. "What on—ah-ah-*aw-choo!*" He sneezed once, then twice, then three times! Before I could grab Goofey, he leaped from Uncle Jack's shoulders and darted out of the family room and through the furnace room door.

Mom spun around. "Goofey!" she yelled, casting accusing eyes at me. "Where is he, Holly?"

"Honest, Mom, I didn't let him out," I said.

I fled to the furnace room to look for Goofey. There I found him crouched on top of a heat duct.

"Please, Goofey," I pleaded, "come down here. You've caused enough trouble already."

He refused to budge. His whiskers twitched as if to say, "I'm not bothering anyone up here, am I?"

Stan came in just then and saw my predicament. "Here, I'll get him for you." He pulled out a stepladder and climbed up, but when he reached for Goofey, the cat slithered away. "Your cat's wreaking havoc with our family night, little sister," he said with a grin—John Wayne style, of course.

"You can say that again," Mom said, peering through the doorway with Carrie at her side.

"Your cat's wreaking havoc with—" Stan began again, but stopped when Mom looked at him cross-eyed.

"Carrie," I said. "Bring Goofey's dish down here with some of his favorite food in it."

"Okay!" She bounded away, giggling.

Mom sent me a stern look, then left to see how Uncle Jack was doing. Meanwhile, Stephie, followed by Mark and Phil, squeezed into the furnace room to watch the excitement.

"I know what'll get him to come down," Phil

said. He rolled his eyes and howled like a hound dog. "Ah-whooo! Rowf! Rowf! Rowf!"

"Oh, *that's* really gonna help," Carrie said as she brought in a dish of tuna-flavored cat food.

Stan took the dish from Carrie and held it up. Sniffing his favorite meal, Goofey inched out, away from the wall, step by kitty step. Slowly, Stan slid the dish down the heat duct as I steadied the ladder.

Stan grunted as he leaned forward. Mark made alien faces, Phil whined softly like a puppy, and Stephie made weird kissy sounds with her lips.

Closer . . . closer . . . Goofey crept toward the dish.

In a flash, Stan grabbed my cat with his free hand. Frightened, Goofey spit and hissed. I snatched up the cat dish just as Stan lost his balance, toppling into a pile of laundry.

And Goofey? He ran for his life!

I chased him upstairs and into my room. And Mom was close behind. She closed the bedroom door firmly behind her.

I was expecting a full-blown lecture, and she didn't disappoint me. "Holly-Heart," she started in, "this is serious business." She stood across the room as I sat huddled with Goofey on my window seat. Her soft blue eyes squinted slightly. "I think it's time you found another home for your cat."

I looked up at her, shocked. "But he's part of our family!"

Mom wasn't listening. "The pills make Jack listless. He's not himself, and I'm really tired of it."

I took a deep breath, thinking of Goofey. And of myself. The purring on my legs rose to a gentle rumble as he relaxed into my lap. I kissed the top of his head.

Mom sat opposite me on the window seat. "Listen, honey, I don't want to make things difficult," she said. "I know how much this cat means to you."

This cat? What a way to refer to the precious bundle of fur who'd seen me through Daddy's leaving and the divorce. Who'd been with me ever since I'd learned to walk . . . and so much more.

"I'm sorry, Holly-Heart." She touched his drowsy head. "My decision has nothing to do with how I feel about Goofey."

"Please, Mom!" I begged. "I'll do anything to keep him here. I'll even make a place in my closet for him when I'm at school. He could eat and drink and sleep in my room, even on weekdays. I promise he'll never go out unless I carry him."

Mom made a sad little sighing sound. My speech had tugged on her heart strings. Perfect!

She stood up to leave. But I could see by her face that I had lost the argument. "Please don't do this, Holly," she said. "I think it's best that Goofey leave. I'm sure you can find a home for him by the end of the weekend."

"But, Mom—"

"I'm sorry," she said and headed down the stairs.

I held my beloved cat close. "It's obvious no one loves you the way I do," I whispered in his tattered ear. "We have to find you a home. One where we can still spend lots of time together."

Pushing my shoe rack aside in my closet, I arranged a soft bed of blankets. "You'll be safe and warm here," I told him.

"Show time," Stan called to me from downstairs.

"Coming," I answered. I didn't feel like watching a silly DVD about pets. But I clumped down the steps anyway, thinking only of Goofey's future.

2

Saturday morning after breakfast, I pulled on my ski jacket, mittens, and scarf.

"Where are you going?" Mom called to me from the kitchen.

"To find a home for an outcast," I announced, running upstairs to get Goofey. I wrapped him in an afghan, and as we came down the steps, I held him up, giving him one last look at his home. "Say 'bye-bye, meow-meow,' to the lamp. Remember, you knocked it over the first Christmas you lived here?"

I glanced toward the kitchen. Could Mom hear my going-away speech?

Going-away parties, after all, were never much fun. Especially if the person . . . er, pet was a close friend like Goofey. He'd shared my window seat, curling up next to me as I wrote in my journal each day. He'd been my companion all through the crazy days of grade school. Not to mention the trials of last year—seventh grade. And Goofey had snuggled near me through every prayer I'd ever prayed, except for the ones prayed in California, where Daddy and his new wife lived.

Staring down at his furry face, I whispered, "How can I say good-bye to you?" A lump sprang up in my throat as I lowered my face to cuddle him.

Just then the front door swung wide. Stephie, Mark, and Phil burst in, followed by Uncle Jack. "It's gonna be a big one," said Uncle Jack, grabbing my shoulders and guiding me to the living room window, Goofey and all. "Look up there. Storm clouds are dying to dump." He pointed to the snow clouds hanging over the mountains. Uncle Jack looked down at the bundle in my arms. "Whatcha got in there?"

Faster than lightning, Goofey hissed and swatted his paw at Uncle Jack's nose. I pulled the cat away.

"Sorry," I said, amazed at the sudden increase in Goofey's intellect. My cat had recognized his own mortal enemy! Not bad for a lazy feline.

Uncle Jack sneezed three times, which brought Mom running. "Holly!" she said as she came into the living room. "I thought you'd already left."

"I'm leaving now." I spun out the front door.

A quick jog down the street brought me to the city bus stop. In a ski village like Dressel Hills, the transportation system was free. Hop on, hop off, anytime—day or night. I pushed my fat friend into the afghan, hiding him. It would be easy to conceal him. Old and pampered, Goofey had slept through longer things than bus rides to my best friend's house.

Soon we were on Andie's street. I pulled the cord and waited for the bus to come to a complete stop before standing up.

Outside, I hurried to the Martinez residence. The wind was picking up, and I kept Goofey covered. "You remember Andie Martinez, don't you, little guy?" I said to the puff of gray nestled in my arms. "She's my best friend ever. If everything goes as planned, she'll be taking very good care of you from now on." I pushed the doorbell with the thumb of my mitten.

Andie's mother opened the door, eyeing my afghan-wrapped bundle. "Quick, come inside, it's whipping up a storm." She hurried through the living room and called up the steps for Andie.

"Be down in a sec," Andie hollered down.

I waited silently, even though Andie's mother cast curious glances at the quiet lump in my arms.

"My toy . . . mine!" a husky shout came from

the kitchen. One of Andie's twin brothers, no doubt. The three-year-olds weren't identical in looks, but their vocal chords definitely had matching decibel levels.

Mrs. Martinez excused herself to investigate the battle, leaving me alone with my precious Goofey. It was sweet having these last few minutes together. Just the two of us. For all too soon, Andie and her family would be the proud new owners of a weird-looking cat named Goofey Meredith.

Meredith's my last name. But Mom traded it to marry Jack Patterson, my deceased aunt's lonely but hilarious husband. That was Thanksgiving, two and a half months ago.

I figured as long as the honeymoon lasted, Goofey was safe. A man like Jack Patterson could take allergy pills off and on, no problem, no complaints. But I'd guessed wrong. Mom was completely bummed out with the medication's side effects. And who could blame her?

"Hey, Holly." Andie appeared wearing dark blue jeans and a black turtleneck sweater. Her dark curly hair framed her chubby cheeks. She eyed the afghan suspiciously. "What's that?"

"We have to talk," I whispered.

She came over and peeked under the afghan. "Oh, it's Goofey," she said. "What's he doing here?"

"It's a long story," I said. "But here's the deal. Goofey's up for adoption, and I'm giving you first chance to—"

"Wait a minute," she interrupted. "I don't want your cat." A look of horror spread across her face. "He's the ugliest thing I've ever seen."

"His looks never bothered you before," I snapped. "All those times at my house—shoot, you even slept with him."

"That's different than claiming him. *You* keep him."

"Can't."

"Why not?"

"Uncle Jack's allergic, and Mom's sick of the pills."

She tried to keep from laughing, but a giggle escaped. "That was so funny at their wedding when your uncle sneezed all over the place. Remember?"

How could I forget?

"Look, I didn't come here to discuss that," I said. "I'm here because I thought you might consider helping me out."

She motioned me up the stairs. Once in her room, she closed the door. Clothes were strewn everywhere. The pink floral comforter had slid halfway off her bed.

"Honestly, Holly," she said, "I'd consider taking your cat for you if I could. It's just that I'm in the middle of real important stuff right now."

I studied her. What was she trying to say?

"I don't know how to tell you this," Andie sat on the floor cross-legged, leaning her back against the bed. Goofey jumped out of the afghan.

"Tell me what?" I asked.

"Well, it's just that . . ." She stopped.

I sat down. "You can tell me anything, Andie," I reassured her. "We've been best friends forever. What is it?"

"Your fourteenth birthday," she said, twisting a dark curl around her finger. "I can't come to your party. It's not that I don't want to; it's just that we're going to Denver Friday evening, and we won't be back in time."

I glared at her. "Why are you telling me this now? The party's a week from today."

"We—my family and I—have been waiting for some paper work," she admitted.

I fumed. "What paper work . . . and what's going on in Denver?"

"Christiana's coming."

"Who?" The way Andie sounded, Christiana might have been the Queen of England or something.

"My pen pal from Austria. Christiana's coming to stay with us for five weeks. It's a private exchange program her parents set up with us."

Andie was silent, like she was waiting for me to respond.

I jumped on it. "Why didn't you tell me this?"

"We didn't know if it was going to work out or not."

I felt totally left out. "When were you going to tell me?"

She shrugged. "Soon enough."

"So you're saying you can't adopt Goofey because of some overseas pen pal? And you're skipping my birthday to pick her up?" I stared at Andie.

"It's just one of those things," she said apologetically. "I'm sure you'll find someone to take your cat. I hope so, Holly, for your sake."

"C'mon, Goofey," I said, rewrapping him in Mom's afghan. "We have to go."

"Sorry. I really am." Andie's face drooped, and she played with her leather watchband.

I headed into the blustery February afternoon without even saying good-bye.

3

By the time the city bus arrived, I felt like a human icicle. Sliding into the first available seat, I cuddled Goofey close. Feelings of frustration swept over me. I couldn't decide which was worse, losing my precious cat, or not having Andie at my birthday party this year.

Without Andie, there was no need for a party. Who wants to celebrate turning fabulous fourteen without your best friend?

I stared out the window. Snowflakes were beginning to fall. Uncle Jack was right; it looked like we were going to get dumped on.

Downtown, the bus stopped to take on more passengers. Paula and Kayla Miller got on, loaded down with shopping bags, probably filled with designer clothes. They wore their brown hair down and straight, matching as always.

"Hey," I said when they saw me.

They sat in the seat behind me. Paula stared at the afghan in my arms. "Did I hear a cat crying?" she asked, flashing her sickening-sweet smile.

Glancing around, I slowly revealed my cat. "This is my homeless pet, Goofey."

Paula's eyes blinked, a week's worth of mascara weighing them down. "He doesn't look homeless to me."

Kayla spoke up. "We heard about Mr. Patterson's allergies. Our father told us."

Paula and Kayla's dad worked with my step-dad in a consulting firm. I wasn't surprised that they'd heard about the problems with Goofey.

"What a shame," Paula cooed over my shoulder, nearly in Goofey's face. "He's so sweet." Then she got up and slid into the seat beside me. "Mind if I pet him?"

"Okay," I lied through my teeth. I didn't want her talking to me, let alone cuddling my cat! This girl had caused me enough trouble to last a lifetime.

I cringed silently as Paula took Goofey from me.

"I've always wanted a cat," she confessed.

And that's not all, I thought. She wanted to take away my boyfriend, Jared Wilkins, too!

Kayla hung over the back of my seat. "He really is cute, in an odd sort of way."

I couldn't bear all this ogling, so I changed the subject. "Where are you two headed?"

"Home," they said in unison.

"We ran into Miss Wannamaker at Plain and Fancy Things," said Kayla. "She's so sweet. We just love her."

Miss W was popular with lots of kids. Whether she taught grammar or creative writing, she made words come alive.

"I think Miss W's in love," Paula continued. "We saw her pricing wedding dresses."

This news was really something for a woman in her fifties who'd never married.

"I think she'd make a fabulous wife," I said. But I was more preoccupied with the twins than with Miss W. I'd made it a point to avoid them ever since they'd moved from Pennsylvania last year. They were so perfect looking and rich it made me sick. They chattered constantly about shopping trips to the mall. Especially Paula. She had a habit of showing off her expensive designer clothes. But worst of all, she'd been after Jared for months. She still glazed over whenever Jared was in close range. And even though he had assured me she wasn't his type, I didn't trust her.

"Is this your street?" Paula asked.

"Uh, yes, it is," I stuttered, turning toward Goofey. Still wrapped in Mom's afghan, he was snuggled against Paula's white fur jacket. I stood up and the bus jolted to a stop. I lurched forward, reaching out to stop my fall.

I felt Paula yank the back of my ski jacket, steadying me. I regained my balance but didn't bother to thank her.

"Downhill Court," announced the driver.

"Coming," I called, reaching for Goofey.

"May I keep him?" Paula pleaded. "Just for a couple of days? I promise to take good care of him."

"You can visit him whenever you want to," Kayla added.

"Please say yes," Paula begged, her violet eyelids blinking at me pitifully.

The driver waited. Passengers jostled grocery bags, young children, and packages. Their faces spelled impatience.

"Okay . . . uh, I guess," I said.

Before the bus doors swooshed shut behind me, I heard Paula say, "I'll call you, Holly."

Oh, fabulous.

Talking on the phone with Paula Miller or her look-alike twin was the last thing I wanted to do. I watched sadly as the bus made its turn onto Aspen Street, carrying with it my little Goofey—in the arms of the enemy.

♥   ♥   ♥

After supper I made a big deal in my journal about losing Goofey. I wrote: *Saturday, February 5: My poor little Goofey is being cared for, right this minute, by strangers. It wouldn't be so bad, but I refuse to set foot in Paula and Kayla Miller's house. And that's where my Goofey is, at least for now. Hopefully I'll persuade Andie to change her mind.*

Christiana-Somebody from Austria is coming to stay with Andie and her family next week. I wonder how it'll work out.

Not every girl is lucky enough to have a Valentine birthday. Daddy always said it meant I was extra special. That's why Mom nicknamed me Holly-Heart. Without Andie, though, the party's a flop.

I closed my journal and sighed. Goofey was gone, and I missed him. Who knows how he was doing, poor, homesick thing. Of course, I could find out in a flash, but it would mean calling Paula Miller. No way.

Curling up on my canopy bed, I stared at my lavender and lace bedroom—private domain regained. It felt good having my room all to myself again, without the super snoopers, Carrie and Stephie. The two of them were roommates now, down the hall.

My sister had reclaimed her old room, the one she'd had before Uncle Jack married Mom. It was great to have Phil and Mark off the second floor and in the new addition on the back of the house. Stan, the oldest of our tribe, took the other bedroom in the addition, vacating the family room. It was a good thing, too. I was tired of having to miss good TV shows just so Stan could pull his bed out of the sofa and lounge around watching John Wayne videos—his latest obsession.

Br-ring! I dashed to the hall, reaching for the phone on the second ring. Too late. Picking it up, I recognized Andie's voice on the line. No doubt she'd called to talk to Stan. They actually liked each other. Mind-boggling.

"Did Holly find a home for Goofey yet?" she asked Stan as I listened.

Dying to hear what he would say, I continued to eavesdrop. "Haven't seen much of Holly today," Stan said. "And . . . who's Goofey?"

Andie laughed.

I wasn't surprised at Stan's remark. He'd never liked Goofey. But it didn't matter. He and I just so happened to be getting along better than ever. I decided to let it go. This time.

Afraid they might hear me breathing, I hung up the phone.

Mom came upstairs just then, dressed in a blue wool sweater, her blond hair pulled back in a gold barrette. "Holly, let's talk." She motioned to my room.

Settling on my bed, she said, "It's almost party time for my birthday girl."

I smoothed the lavender quilted comforter. "Yeah, it's countdown to nothing much."

"What about the make-over party we planned? Sounds like fun, doesn't it?"

"Who cares," I grumbled.

"But Jack and I—"

"Please don't make plans behind my back," I snapped. "Honestly, I feel like calling the whole birthday thing off."

"Holly-Heart," she protested, "what's happened?"

I got up and wandered across the room. Without looking at her, I blurted, "Andie won't be coming."

"Well, why not?"

"She has plans. With Christiana of Austria." I grabbed Bearie-O, Andie's teddy bear, off the shelf. Hugging him, I told Mom about Andie's pen pal and the exchange they'd planned.

"Does this mean Andie will go to Austria next summer?"

I hadn't thought of that. Andie was probably holding out that tidbit of information for a later date. Unpredictable Andie, always full of surprises! Not always happy ones, either.

"It's not easy having a best friend who can't even tell you the important stuff ahead of time."

I squeezed the stuffed bear extra hard.

Mom came over and sat near me on the window seat. "This has you very upset, Holly. If you'd like, we could arrange to have the party on Monday, your actual birthday." She sighed. "Could Andie come then?"

"She'll be up to her eyeballs introducing Christiana to Dressel Hills by that time," I responded. "I can see it now—"

Mom interrupted. "Holly-Heart, I don't like the sound of this. I think you're jealous."

"Isn't that a shame," I said sarcastically. "And I haven't even met Andie's friend yet."

Mom stood up. "Be careful you don't let these feelings come between you and Andie. It would be a sad thing for a lifelong friendship to be marred by your bad attitude."

Mom's lecture bored me. I knew all that stuff. What I didn't know was how I could possibly fit in with Andie when Christiana arrived.

As far as I was concerned, second best might as well be zero!

4

Sunday morning I slept in longer than I should have. Through a sleepy haze, I rubbed my eyes. Bearie-O, the droopy-eyed teddy bear Andie had traded with me for mine in first grade, stared down at me from the shelf near my window seat. Since Goofey was gone, I'd have to revert back to my childhood and sleep with Bearie-O. It was an option, at least.

Getting up, I hurried for the shower. On the way, I noticed Mom's bedroom door open. For a moment I stood, listening. It was unmistakable. Classical music wafted down the hall, interspersed with the clinking of fine silver against china. Could it be?

I strained to listen, inching my way down the hallway. Mixed with the music was soft laughter. Uncle Jack was serving Mom breakfast in bed!

How romantic, I thought, making my way to

the bathroom. *Someday* . . .

I allowed my mind to wander. Jared Wilkins, the first real crush of my life, instantly came to mind. Lathering up, I thought of someone else, too—Sean Hamilton. Hundreds of miles distanced us. Tall, tan, and very mature, Sean lived in Southern California, just down the beach from Daddy.

Sometimes I regretted not meeting him on Christmas Eve for a walk on the seashore. It had sounded so dreamy. Maybe he had just wanted to be friends, but now I would never know.

My dad was probably right. *"Develop lots of friendships with guys,"* he'd said when I visited at Christmas. *"There's plenty of time for romance later."*

Andie didn't agree when I told her about my talk with Daddy at Christmas. "What's wrong with a little mushy stuff?" she'd said, laughing.

I grabbed a towel and hopped out of the shower. My thoughts went back to Sean and the moonlit walk I'd missed. Daydreaming about the possibilities, I didn't hear the knock on my door.

"Holly, I have to go. Hurry up!" It was Carrie.

"Okay, okay." I reached for my robe. Little sisters!

♥　　♥　　♥

As was our custom since Uncle Jack married Mom, we attended the early service at church on Sundays. Today I asked permission to sit with Andie. Usually, all eight of us filled up one long pew. Mom liked it that way: family togetherness in worship. But I needed space.

Sitting next to Andie and her entire family, I sensed something was wrong. I could feel the tension. And she seemed preoccupied, probably with her pen pal's arrival.

"A cat like Goofey would make a fabulous contribution to Christiana's stay in America," I whispered in her ear, then reached for the hymnal.

She fluffed her short, springy curls. "I know you love your pet, Holly," she said, "but why don't you let Paula adopt him?"

Paula? How did she know?

"Would you want someone you love spending day in and day out at the Miller residence?" I whispered.

She shrugged halfheartedly, like she wasn't really listening.

I couldn't talk about how I disliked the Miller twins—not in church, of all places. So I sat there fuming about everything imaginable. Goofey staying at Paula's . . . and Miss Christiana So-and-So living at Andie's!

♥   ♥   ♥

Jared waited for me in the church aisle after the benediction. His dark hair was combed back neatly, and his eyes lit up when he saw me. "Hey, Holly. You look great today."

I blushed. "Thanks." He looked fine himself, wearing a blue cotton shirt and khakis.

"Coming to youth service Thursday?" he asked.

"Wouldn't miss it." I couldn't help grinning. Jared was so easy to be around. Then an idea struck me. "Uh, Jared," I said hesitantly, "how would you like to adopt my cat?"

Jared scratched his head and stuffed his hands into his pockets. "I have a problem . . . with cats," he admitted.

"What's that supposed to mean?" I felt rejected. "Cats are fabulous," I told him. "I'd have a dozen of them if I could."

He smiled that adorable smile, but it didn't do a thing for me. Not today. "I'm a dog person," he said proudly.

His comment ticked me off. "Can't you at least keep Goofey for a little while?" I pleaded. "It'll buy me some time."

"Holly," he said, as an exasperated frown appeared. "It wouldn't be fair to your cat—

hanging out with someone like me."

"But you're my friend," I argued. "I should be able to count on you no matter what."

"Hey, friends can't bail each other out *all* the time," he said. "You should know that."

"He's right." Paula Miller sidled up to us. "Only God can do that. He's the only one who can be there for us all the time."

I glared at her. *Who asked you?* I thought, watching her like a hawk, especially since she seemed to be showing off her new dress. Probably for Jared's benefit. He straightened his collar while Paula flashed another Colgate smile.

Grudgingly, I asked Paula how my cat was doing. Even though I disliked her, I loved Goofey.

"Oh, Goofey's just fine." Paula grinned wider than ever. "He's absolutely wonderful."

"That's nice," I whispered. But I wasn't so sure. If Goofey had any good taste, he'd hate being around Paula.

Just then, out of the corner of my eye, I noticed Andie and her family leaving by the side door. "I'll see you tomorrow," I said abruptly to Jared and Paula, hurrying to catch up with Andie.

I spotted her in the parking lot, heading toward her car. "Andie, wait!"

She stopped and turned around. "This better

not be about that cat of yours."

"It's about my birthday party. Can you come if I change the day?"

Her dark curls blew against her face. "To when?"

"Valentine's Day, a week from tomorrow." I realized I was holding my breath, waiting for her response.

"I'll have to let you know," she said. Then she hurried to catch up with her family.

♥　♥　♥

I called Paula on Sunday night and then again on Monday after school. I simply had to know how Goofey was. I missed him terribly.

"Oh, hello, Holly," Paula cooed when she answered the phone.

Carrying the portable phone, I paced nervously around my bedroom. "How's Goofey eating?"

"Very well, and Kayla thinks he's beginning to bond with me. I've been giving him lots of attention, including a bath every day. He loves the rose-scented bubbles."

I couldn't believe my ears. "You're kidding! He likes bubble baths?"

"Oh yes," she said. "And I'm making him some little pajamas to wear at night."

I gasped. "Pajamas?" *Probably designer pj's.*

"They're darling. You should come over and see them."

"Um, sometime." I switched the phone to my other ear. "But you don't have to sew him pajamas, Paula. I only wanted you to keep him until I could—"

"Oh no, no!" she exclaimed. "Please don't take Goofey away."

Oh, puh-leeze. This was too much!

"I couldn't stand the thought of losing him," she insisted.

"Hey, I know the feeling," I said. "I'll be right over."

It was time to put a stop to this bonding Paula Miller had going on with my cat. Rushing downstairs, I swung open the coat closet in the front hall. My pink-and-purple ski jacket was handy, so I flung it on.

"Where are you going?" Carrie said, looking up from her book. She was snuggled up on the sofa in the living room.

"None of your business."

"We might be gone when you get back. Uncle Jack's taking us to get fitted for our own skis," Carrie said.

"He is?"

"Yep, we're going skiing soon. He wants each of us to have our own equipment." Carrie slouched against the sofa. "Isn't it great having a rich uncle in the family?" Then she burst into giggles.

"You're a nut case," I said, looking around for Mom and Uncle Jack. "They'll hear you."

"It's no secret. Do you know how much money we have?" She stared at me. "Well, *do* you?"

"What are you talking about?"

Carrie motioned to me with her pointer finger. "How do you think we paid for the addition on the house?"

"Uncle Jack did, of course. Who else?" I sat on the arm of the sofa.

"Last night I heard him telling Mom about the money he got when Aunt Marla died. You won't believe it," she said, her eyes sparkling.

"People get insurance money when their spouses die. It's no big deal."

"Half a million dollars is a big deal." Carrie shoved her finger into her book, marking the page. "How much is that?"

"Figure it out." I leaped up and dashed out the door. *Whoa, she wasn't kidding. We were rich, all right!*

Carrie's news cast a spell over everything in my path. Running down the street toward Paula

Miller's house, I felt strange. No wonder Uncle Jack had tripled my allowance. It was nice of him, but really, kids my age didn't need that much money. I was putting most of it in the church offering. In fact, last Sunday before the service I'd stopped by the church bulletin board in the foyer and studied a display of missionaries and their families. I wanted to support one of them, but I wasn't sure whom. Then another picture had caught my eye—of a thin, naked child, crying from hunger. I resolved right there to use my allowance to help starving children, too.

Just ahead, the Miller twins' house came into view. Set on the side of a hill, the house was in one of the lah-dee-dah-est areas of Dressel Hills.

I groaned as I made my way up the steep driveway, praying. *Dear Lord, if Carrie's right about the money, please don't let me become like Paula Miller—constantly buying new clothes and living for the next shopping spree. I want to help people with my money, not hoard it to myself.*

When I rang the doorbell, it played some long excerpt from Mozart or Beethoven, I wasn't sure which. Anyway, I was surprised when Paula answered the door. Minus Goofey.

"Won't you please come in?" Paula said, opening the door wide. She showed me into the large foyer, where a wide velvet tapestry of an English garden graced the wall. Fresh roses, yellow as buttercups, brightened a cherrywood table nearby.

"Where's Goofey?" I asked, gazing overhead at a twinkling glass chandelier.

"Upstairs," she said.

I sneaked a peek at the living room as we headed for the curved staircase. Lily-white chairs and sofas were dotted with satiny pillows of black and red. A slate-black coffee table held a tall, white vase bulging with silk crimson roses. At the top of the curved staircase, Paula's room awaited, filled with the scent of woodland potpourri.

"Kayla's resting, so let's keep our voices low," Paula suggested.

What century was she born in? I wondered, amazed at the golden Cinderella-like mirror hanging over her dresser. The floral print bed-spread of pastel blues and greens perfectly matched the wallpaper and the throw pillows on two powder-blue easy chairs.

"Would you care for a soda?" Paula offered.

I nodded. "Sure, thanks."

Paula opened a miniature refrigerator near her closet and pulled out a Coke. "I hope it's cold enough."

I took the soda and thanked her. A *refrigerator* in her *room?* What else did this girl have— diamonds and pearls in her jewelry box, maybe?

Paula directed me to one of her soft chairs. "Wait here while I get Goofey up from his nap," she said.

Goofey had been spoiled rotten at my house, but this. . . ! I took a sip of my soda, surveying the picture-perfect view. Getting up, I went to the window and leaned my knee on the padded window seat, in awe of the mountainous sight. Looking down, I caught my breath. A window seat? Paula had a window seat just like mine.

I don't know why her having a window seat bothered me, but it did. For some reason I didn't want to have a single thing in common with this girl. Absolutely nothing!

"Here we are," Paula said cheerfully, returning with Goofey in her arms. "Isn't he simply adorable?" she cooed. Cooing was one of her trademarks. Hers and Kayla's.

"Simply," I echoed. "Now, what's this about bubble baths?"

"Oh, that," she waved her hand as though it was an ordinary thing for a cat to take bubble baths. "Would you like to witness it for yourself?"

"Now?" It was hard to believe that's all Paula could dream up for after-school entertainment. What about friends? Didn't she have anyone besides her twin sister to hang out with?

"Goofey really loves his baths," she continued. "I'll draw his water now if you'd like."

"Actually, I'd rather just play with him if you don't mind." I really wanted to take him back home where he belonged. But Mom would never hear of it. If only I could talk some sense into Andie. Or Jared.

Paula put Goofey down. He stood close to her for a moment, then wandered over to nuzzle my leg. Stooping down, I picked him up. He smelled like roses. Probably the bubble bath variety.

"I've missed you," I whispered. Purring contentedly, Goofey rubbed his head against my chin.

"If it would make you feel any better," Paula

said, "I'd be delighted to purchase him from you."

"Buy my Goofey?" I was still shocked that the facts hadn't sunk into her brain. "Goofey's not for sale. He's only here for a few days, like we agreed."

"I really wish—"

"Well, I have to be going," I interrupted. "I've got important stuff to take care of."

"You can't stay?" She sounded disappointed.

"Sorry," I said. Then I gave Goofey a kiss on his pink nose and left the room. "He's yours till Wednesday."

"Wednesday?" she asked. "What happens then?"

"I'll find a permanent home by then," I said.

Paula followed me down the long staircase. "Thank you, Holly, for allowing me this time with your darling cat."

This girl is about as flaky as a Barbie doll, I thought as she opened the front door.

"Remember, Holly, you're welcome to visit Goofey any time," she said as I stepped out into the cold.

I turned to face her and noticed with a shock that her eyes looked misty, like she was about to cry. "Thanks," I said uncomfortably, eager to get away before she started bawling on my shoulder. "I'll come get Goofey in two days."

"Rest assured, I'll take good care of him for you," she said as I headed down the flagstone steps toward the tree-lined street.

A twinge of guilt haunted me on my walk home. It was rude the way I'd treated Paula. I'd called her rotten things like *pathetic* and *pitiful* behind her back. But her only real problem was she was different. *Very* different.

When I finally arrived home, the gray van was gone, which meant only one thing: Carrie was right about Uncle Jack spending big bucks on the family. I loved to ski, but somehow I couldn't picture Mom on the slopes. Guess Uncle Jack was opening new horizons for her.

Instead of going into the house, I hopped on the city bus. With any luck I'd link up with my family at the sporting goods store.

On the bus I spotted Mrs. Martinez seated near the front.

"Hello there, Holly!" she called.

I hurried to take a seat beside her. "Andie told me about the guest you have coming next weekend."

She smiled. "We're excited about having Christiana in our home. From her letters, she seems like a lovely young lady."

And I'm not? The resentful thought jagged across my mind. I forced it out of my head. "Sounds like fun," I lied.

"Andie has been wanting to do something like this for quite some time now."

Funny, she hadn't told *me* about it.

"She hopes to learn from Christiana while she's here, and if things work out, Andie may spend some time in Austria next year."

So Mom guessed right. Why was I not surprised?

"Well, tell Andie hi for me." I stood up when I saw the doughnut shop next to the sporting goods store. "Here's where I get off."

"Nice seeing you, Holly," she said.

"You too, Mrs. Martinez." I hurried off the bus and headed into the sporting goods store. Sure enough, my family was there. All of them.

Carrie and Stephie were modeling matching yellow ski outfits, completely ignoring the price tags. Mom was trying on ski boots, and the boys were off in another corner of the store checking out the most expensive skis.

This bothered me. A lot. There were tons of starving children in the world, and here we were spending zillions on ski outfits.

"Holly, I'm glad you found us," Mom said, looking up as she buckled the shiny ski boots. "What do you think?" She held her foot up.

"I can't believe you're actually going to hit the slopes." I was laughing. But not at the pricey boots she wore.

Uncle Jack sat next to her, wrapping his arm around her. "She'll have plenty of time now for sports and leisure activities," he said with a twinkle in his eye.

"Mom's quitting work, right?" I said gleefully. All this money in the family had its advantages, after all.

"Yep, and she's going to join an aerobics club to get back in shape," Carrie announced.

"She's not that much out of shape," I defended Mom.

"Thanks, Holly-Heart," Mom said, touching my hand.

Uncle Jack led me to the shelf displaying boots my size. I picked up the cheapest pair.

"Those might make it down the hill twice." Uncle Jack chuckled. He picked up another pair. "Now, here's something that'll last a good long time."

Eyeing the price tag, I said, "But they cost so much!"

Uncle Jack sat me down near Mom and helped me slip on the boots. "It's better to pay a few more dollars and have them last for several seasons," he explained. "Besides, your feet have stopped growing. Who knows how long you'll be stuck wearing these."

I could see his point. Still, I couldn't get that picture of the starving child out of my mind.

6

Wednesday in science class, Andie was so engrossed in taking notes she scarcely noticed me. After class, she stayed to talk to Mr. Ross, our teacher. A major switcheroo.

I waited as long as I could at her locker. Finally giving up, I headed off for English. Miss Wannamaker looked thinner, like she was losing weight. I was curious about that. Was she trying to impress Mr. Ross?

Jared slid into the desk across the aisle. "Hey, Holly-Heart. Got your homework done?" He flashed that wonderful warm smile.

"It's right here." I patted my school bag.

"I hear we're having a visitor from Austria."

"Yep. That's all Andie's talking about." I searched for my English book in my bag. Miss W was getting ready to begin class. "See you at lunch, okay?"

"Perfect," he said, using my word. When he winked at me, my heart did its usual wild flip-flop.

♥　　♥　　♥

At noon, Paula slipped into the hot-lunch line behind me. "You should see Goofey in his new pajamas," she purred. "He looks so adorable."

"You sewed them already?"

"They weren't difficult," she said, tossing her hair back over her shoulder. "I followed the pattern for a doggie sweater."

"You what?"

"I crochet," she explained. "It's lots of fun."

I could just see it now—my Goofey in pink poodle pajamas. It was enough to give me a hissy fit. "Poor thing," I muttered under my breath.

"He seems to like it," she said, following me to the table where Andie sat saving places for both Jared and me.

"Mind if I join you?" Paula asked, holding her tray till I answered.

I studied Andie, still writing notes. "Hey,

relax, it's lunchtime," I teased, motioning for Paula to sit on the other side of me.

Andie kept her nose stuck in a book.

"Whatcha studying?" I asked, peering over at Andie and her mammoth book.

"Stuff about western Europe," she said without looking up.

"Oh, I know. You want to communicate with your new friend, right?"

"She speaks English fluently. Started studying it in fifth grade."

Paula leaned forward, talking around me. "What does she know about Colorado?"

"I've already described Dressel Hills to her, if that's what you mean." Andie looked up momentarily.

"And what about when you go over there?" I asked. "What then?"

Andie closed her book. "Well, if things work out, I should have enough money saved by a year from now." She had a faraway look in her brown eyes. "I want to travel the world. See the sights, meet different people."

"It's a good goal for you," I said, not realizing it sounded like a put-down till it was out of my mouth.

Andie ignored the comment, or maybe her head was in a cloud somewhere in the Alps. "Mr.

Ross is giving me extra-credit work to help pull up my science grade. My parents said if I work extra hard this semester they'll help me with my plane fare—to visit Christiana."

"Wow, sounds like you're serious about this," I said.

Andie leaned on the table, looking at Paula on the other side of me. "So . . . how do you like Holly's cat so far?"

Paula was munching on a hot dog. "Uhmm," she mumbled, wiping her lips.

It was the first unintelligible remark Paula had made since she moved here last April.

"Her mouth's full," I explained.

We both waited for her to swallow. At last she said she'd been praying about Goofey's well-being. That the right person would end up with him.

Man, this is getting nutty, I thought. *Paula's talking to God about my cat.*

"You sound like Holly," Andie said, chuckling. "She prays about things like that. And you know what's amazing? God answers her prayers."

I spooned up some chili for my hot dog. "But sometimes the answer is 'not yet' or just plain 'no.'"

"Which reminds me," Andie said. "About

next week and your birth—"

I made a cut-throat gesture for her to stop talking. Paula had *not* been invited to my party. This could be embarrassing.

Andie glanced down awkwardly, playing with her napkin. Then she said, "I've gotta run. Stan has a book he bought in Germany last summer. I'm supposed to meet him at his locker. See ya."

I knew by the look on her face she wasn't coming to my party no matter when I was having it. I just hoped Paula hadn't heard. She was the last person I wanted hanging around.

Now . . . what to do about Goofey? There was no changing Andie's mind. That was obvious. She seemed determined not to have anything to do with my cat. On the other hand, here was Paula, a girl who loved him almost as much as I did.

I needed some time to think. What I really needed was a backup plan. So I mentioned my preliminary idea to Paula, who was finishing her lunch. "Do you think you could keep Goofey for a few more days?"

Her face broke into a grin. "Do you mean it?"

You would've thought she'd just won a shopping spree.

"Only a few more days," I said, "till I can work something out."

She sighed. "Oh my! How can I ever thank you, Holly?"

"I'll think of a way," I said a bit too sarcastically.

Jared showed up just then, and Paula excused herself promptly. Strange. If I hadn't known better, I would have thought Paula was trying to avoid Jared. How weird was that?

"Heard you have a cat for sale," Jared said, sitting beside me.

I bristled at his remark. "I would never part with Goofey for money," I declared. "I couldn't possibly put a price tag on him."

"You're one loyal and dedicated owner." He smeared mustard, ketchup, and mayonnaise all over his hot dog. "Paula seems to love him, too," he said. "Why don't you let her keep him?"

"Never in a zillion years," I said.

Jared shot me a surprised look. I didn't want to explain why I disliked Paula, so I made a point of looking at my watch.

"Going somewhere?" he asked.

"I need to pick up some library books before my next class. Wanna come?"

He held up his hot dog. "I'll catch up with you later."

"Okay. See ya." I rushed off to the library, hoping to find a book on Austria. Then just maybe I could get Andie's attention. Finally!

7

Paula called after school. "Something's wrong with Goofey," she said, her voice quivering.

I gripped the phone. "What do you mean?"

"He's acting very strange," she answered. "He won't eat, and he's throwing up. I called the vet."

"What did the vet say?" I tugged on my hair nervously.

"He said to bring him into the animal clinic right away."

"Thanks for telling me, Paula. I'll get Stan to drive me. I'll meet you there." I hung up the phone, trembling as I dashed down the steps to the main level.

What had Paula done to my precious kitty?

"Stan!" I called.

No answer.

"Where is he?" I said through clenched

teeth, disgusted at his lack of immediate response. "Stan!" I called again. Louder this time.

Carrie and Stephie came running upstairs. "Stan's gone," Stephie said.

"Yeah, he left a while ago," Carrie informed me.

"Just great," I muttered, wishing the city bus route went as far as the vet's. What could I do?

The TV blared in the family room downstairs. Maybe Mark knew something. I dashed down another flight of stairs. Carrie and Stephie followed. "When's your dad coming home?" I asked Mark.

"How should I know?" he blurted, making one of his disgusting alien faces at me. Stephie giggled.

"Doesn't anybody know anything around here?" I shrieked, growing more irritated by the second. "Goofey's in trouble, and I have to see him before—"

"Before what?" Carrie asked, her eyes ready to pop.

"He's sick, really sick, and I have to get to the vet's. Goofey will be scared if I'm not there," I said, tears blurring my vision.

"Is . . . is he gonna die?" Stephie cried.

A hideous thought. One I couldn't bear to face. "I hope not," I answered.

Running upstairs to the kitchen, I reached for the portable phone. Maybe Andie's mom could drive me across town.

♥ ♥ ♥

Andie answered on the first ring.

"Is your mom home?" I asked.

"She's out buying groceries for next weekend when Christiana comes," she said.

"Oh, I just thought maybe she could drive me somewhere. Goofey's real sick . . . at the vet's. I need to get there somehow."

"What about Stan? Can't he drive you?"

"Stan's not here and Mom's gone. I wish I could drive!" It looked hopeless for transportation. And Goofey needed me. No one else could give him the kind of love and attention he needed now.

"Sorry, Holly. Wish I could help," she said.

"I'll work something out." I said good-bye and hung up.

In desperation I grabbed the phone book and called a cab. It would probably eat up every dime of my mission project, but it was well worth it to be with Goofey.

I dashed back to the family room, informing

Mark and the girls where I was headed.

"Mommy won't be happy about this," Carrie said. "You're supposed to be in charge of us while she's gone."

"Don't worry," Mark said, "I'll make sure nothing bad happens."

I eyed him. "That's what I'm afraid of."

"We'll sit right here and watch Mark make alien faces till Mommy comes home," Stephie said. "We promise."

Mark started his gross facial repertoire.

"You're hopeless," I said, turning toward the stairs.

The cab pulled into the driveway just as I stepped onto the porch. I hurried to get in.

Rush-hour traffic was appalling in a ski resort in winter. We weaved in and out of traffic on Aspen Street. Afternoon skiers were coming off the slopes in droves. The latest snowfall provided the perfect conditions—packed powder.

"Can you go a different way?" I pleaded with the driver.

"We're almost out of the worst," he said. "What's your hurry?"

I told him about Goofey.

"Maybe he caught a simple flu bug," the cabbie offered.

"Flu can be deadly for a cat as old as Goofey," I said, praying silently.

When we arrived at the vet's, I paid the cab fare and made my way up the snowy steps to the animal clinic. Inside, Paula sat on the edge of her chair.

"Where's Goofey?" I asked.

"The vet took him in there." She pointed to a door across from us. I noticed her eyes glistening.

I didn't wait to hear more. Making a beeline for the door, I darted inside, looking for my cat.

"May I help you, dear?" It was the vet's assistant, peering over the top of her granny glasses. She was filling out some papers. I saw "Goofey Meredith" written at the top of one of them.

"I'm Holly Meredith," I replied. "Goofey belongs to me."

Slowly, she removed her glasses. "Please sit down." She motioned to a vacant chair.

A giant lump crowded my throat. I could almost predict what she would say. Goofey is dying. It will be a slow, painful death, unless . . . No! No way would I let them put my darling Goofey to sleep.

I studied the woman momentarily, then blurted, "What's wrong with my cat?"

The woman smiled sweetly. "We're doing everything possible for him," she said. "He has a severe intestinal problem, caused by ingesting large amounts of soap. Actually, bubble bath."

I took a deep breath. Paula was the person responsible for poisoning my cat! Wanting to scream, I managed to force polite words out of my mouth. "May I see Goofey now?"

"Certainly." The assistant led me into another room. She explained that the technician was giving Goofey liquid charcoal to absorb the soap in his stomach. I watched, willing the tears back, trying to focus my eyes on Goofey.

"We'll have to keep your cat for several days," the technician said.

"What for?" I asked.

"We'll put a tube down his stomach for starters, and after a while he should be as good as new. But you'll have to help us," he said, smiling.

"I'll do anything," I said, inching closer to the gray form lying deathly still on the table.

"You'll have to monitor his eating and drinking habits for a week after we release him. I'll give you a prescription for Goofey—fifty milligrams of Amoxicillin, twice a day. In addition to that, he'll need an anti-inflammatory to make sure the liquid charcoal doesn't irritate his stomach." He stood up and walked me to the door. "I'll make a list of things for you to follow."

"Thank you very much for saving Goofey's life," I said, following him to the waiting area.

"Well, you can be sure we'll give him the best of care," he said. "But when he's released, it would be a good idea if Goofey returns to his home." He glanced at Paula just then. "He'll get well much more quickly if he's surrounded by those he's accustomed to."

Another lump swelled in my throat. This was turning into a nightmare.

After the vet left, I glared at Paula. "Thanks for trying to kill my cat," I whispered.

Paula wiped a tear. "I never thought . . . it's just so awful . . . I'm truly sorry, Holly. I really am."

I couldn't stand her blubbering. I turned to the receptionist's desk. "May I use your phone, please?" I asked.

The phone rang twice before Uncle Jack answered. "I'll be right there," he said after I told him my dilemma.

Thanking the receptionist for the use of her phone, I turned around. Paula was gone. *She's out of here for good*, I thought, seething silently as I waited for Uncle Jack.

Then I heard a familiar cooing sound coming from the open door. I stood up. Yep, it was Paula's voice all right. Who could mistake it?

Moving closer, I peeked around the doorway and saw Paula standing near my cat, stroking him. Furious, I headed down the hall toward her. "Don't touch my cat!" I said.

Paula jumped. "But I had to say good-bye to

Goofey," she sputtered, eyes a-flutter.

"Well, you said it, now disappear."

She looked at me sorrowfully. "Oh, Holly, please forgive me. I wouldn't hurt Goofey for anything."

"Well, you did, and it can't be changed." The angry words surprised me as they tumbled out.

Paula rushed past me, sobbing.

I said my good-byes to Goofey in private. His fur smelled of roses, the scent that Paula had been smothering him with every day. He didn't move, or purr, or anything. His eyes were glazed over, unseeing.

"Please get well," I whispered, touching his tattered ear. "I can't live without you."

8

Settling into the bucket seat of Uncle Jack's van, I thanked him for picking me up.

He apologized all over the place about what had happened. "I'm sorry it had to be my allergies that sent Goofey away."

I wouldn't let him take the blame. "It's not your fault. You couldn't help it."

He offered to pay for the entire bill. "Don't worry another second about this, Holly," he said. "That's what stepdads are for, right?" He grinned at me.

"Thanks," I said, still unsettled about what to do when Goofey was well enough to come home. If only Andie would agree to keep him, the problem would be solved.

♥   ♥   ♥

After supper, Mom and Uncle Jack went to Bible study. I spent the evening doing pre-algebra with Stan. He assisted me, with occasional comments from "John Wayne."

When the phone rang, I hoped it was Andie, not Paula.

I got my wish.

"Hey," Andie said. "What're you doing Friday night?"

"Nothing much," I replied.

"C'mon, Holly, you sound morbid," she scolded. "You'll have a very cool make-over party."

"Don't rub it in." I felt a sickening lump in the pit of my stomach. She was ruining everything by not coming.

"Relax," Andie said in her quirkiest voice. "I'm still invited, right?"

I almost dropped the phone. "What are you saying?"

"Christiana's arriving earlier than we thought. We're picking her up on Friday morning."

"So you can come?"

"I'll come if Christiana's invited, too." It was more of a question than a statement.

"Do you think, I mean, will she be comfortable attending a stranger's birthday party on her first night in America?" I asked.

"Oh sure," Andie said. "She'll have a great time meeting you and Amy-Liz. Who else is invited?"

"Joy and Shauna are coming . . . and that's it," I said, thinking about Paula Miller, who didn't even know about the party. No way was the cat killer invited.

"That's six of us," she said. "It's best to have an even number at parties, my mom always says. That way no one feels left out."

I laughed. "My mom says the same thing."

"How much makeup should we bring?" she asked.

"Don't worry about it. We'll have everything we need here."

"I'll bring my new cucumber mask," she said. "You have to try it. It's so organic and earthy."

"I can't wait, now that you're coming. And guess what? Mom's hired a beautician for the party. We'll have our hair restyled after we experiment with makeup. Cool, huh?"

"Great! I want my hair straightened for a change," she said, laughing. "What about you? Gonna get your hair chopped?"

"Styled," I said. "Not cut."

"I've never seen you with short hair," she said. "Bet you'd look cute."

Here we were having this fabulous conversation, and she had to bring *that* up. She knew better. Never in a zillion years would I cut my hair.

"How long is Christiana's hair?" I asked, changing the subject.

"A little longer than chin length, according to her pictures. It's close to your hair color, Holly."

So that's why she mentioned getting my hair cut. She was thinking of her pen pal. Again.

"Guess what happened today?" I said.

"Something about your cat?" she asked casually.

"Yeah, Paula tried to kill him!"

"And you're upset."

"Upset, nothing. I'm furious at Paula. It's her fault."

"What actually happened?" Andie was all ears.

I told her about the daily bubble baths, how Goofey had swallowed lots of the soap, making him sick.

"Never heard of giving a cat a bath," she said. "Don't they lick themselves clean?"

"Of course. Anybody knows that."

"Well, Paula's different, you know."

"No kidding," I said, the anger boiling up again.

"Well, I'll see you tomorrow," she said. "I've gotta get my room ready for Christiana."

"Okay, see you."

I hung up, feeling both happy and worried. Andie would be at my party, but so would a complete stranger. One that I'd already decided to dislike.

Suddenly a new thought struck me. *What if Christiana doesn't like me?*

♥ ♥ ♥

Thursday after school, Stan drove me to see Goofey. Andie rode along, sitting between Stan and me. So far, Andie was hanging on to this boyfriend longer than most.

"What'll happen to Goofey when he's released from the clinic?" Stan asked. "Who will take care of him then?"

I glanced at Andie. Maybe hearing the words from Stan would increase my chances of persuading her to adopt him. "Good question," I said. "There's no way I want Paula getting close to him again."

"What's so bad about Paula?" Stan teased.

"Just because she's rich and gorgeous doesn't mean she can take care of cats," Andie joked back.

"Says who?" Stan said, pulling into the parking lot behind the clinic.

Andie elbowed him in the ribs.

"Coming in?" I asked, unlocking the car door.

"You betcha," Andie said.

Stan waved playfully as we headed inside.

Goofey had a tube in his stomach, so he couldn't have visitors. Besides, the technician probably didn't want to gross us out. "Your friend was here today," he said.

"Who?"

"Your friend Paula Miller. She came around lunchtime."

What gall! It made me madder than ever. But I covered it well. "Make sure you tell Goofey I love him," I said. "Say my name in his ear three times every hour."

His eyebrows shot up. "No problem," he said with a grin.

"You're crazy, Holly," Andie said on the way back to the car.

"So what? Doctors prescribe medicine in double and triple doses, don't they?"

She opened the car door. "Cats don't understand English, do they?"

I waited for her to slide in next to Stan. "They're smarter than you think." I wanted to say, *Why don't you adopt Goofey and find out?* But I bit my tongue and decided I'd pray for an adoptive parent for him instead.

♥ ♥ ♥

Back home I wrote in my journal. A longer entry than usual. The final paragraph read: *Tomorrow's my birthday party and Andie's coming! (So is Christiana, but I'll get over it, I guess.)*

I hid my diary in the bottom drawer. It felt good reclaiming every inch of this room. Opening my closet, I chose a clean outfit for youth service.

After supper, Stan and I headed off to church. When we arrived, Paula and Kayla were walking up the steps. "Go with me to the side door," I pleaded to Stan.

He frowned and turned on his John Wayne charm. "What's the matter, little sister?"

"Paula's pathetic," I muttered.

"Now there's an interesting Christian attitude." He held the door as I trudged inside.

"If I never see Paula's face again, I'll be thrilled," I said.

And then . . . around the corner she appeared. "I have to talk to you, Holly," she said, reaching for my arm.

I backed away, ready to do battle.

Then Stan stepped in front of me. John Wayne's voice rang through the hall. "Listen here, pilgrim. This here's the sanctuary of God.

I'd suggest you take your fight outside." He took Paula's arm by the elbow, guiding her away from my wrath. She looked up at him, smiling with all her teeth. "Well, Missy, looks like I saved your hide," Stan said as they strolled down the hall.

I watched as Stan and the cat killer turned the corner in the foyer. Inching my way forward, I peeked around.

"Seems as though what we've got here is just a little misunderstanding," John Wayne droned on.

Paula, the cat poisoner, giggled just as Andie appeared at the top of the steps, face-to-face with Stan. With his arm around Paula!

9

Andie's eyes popped. "Excuse me?" she demanded.

Not given to defeat, Stan came up with the perfect comeback. "Missy," he turned to Paula. "Like I said, life's full of little misunderstandings."

Gallantly, he offered his other elbow to Andie. "Well, pilgrims, let's go to church."

Sparks flew from Andie's dark eyes as she caught my glance. Stan was in for it now.

Paula's giggling diminished to a grin as she released her hold on my cousin. "Thanks for everything, Mister. See ya at the roundup."

Some pathetic imitation, I thought, as she turned around and caught my eye.

"Holly, I really do need to talk to you." She was coming at me, full speed.

I stood my ground. "There's nothing to say."

I pushed past her as Andie grabbed Stan and pulled him into the youth service.

After we sang some contemporary praise and worship choruses, Pastor Rob stood up. "Tonight we're going to divide into small groups, but first the devotional." He read the Scripture from Matthew 5:44. " 'But I tell you: Love your enemies and pray for those who persecute you . . .' "

Some text.

If I hadn't known better, I would've thought Stan or someone else had filled in Pastor Rob on what was going on between Paula and me.

He continued to talk about the verse, skillfully weaving the Scripture into a devotional. When it was time to divide into discussion groups, Pastor Rob had us count off by fives. I was a two. So was Paula. Quickly, I disappeared into the girls' bathroom and stayed there till I was sure the small group stuff was over.

At last I came out, only to find Paula waiting beside the closed chapel doors. "I know you're angry at me," she said, "and I don't blame you. But I honestly didn't know bubble baths would harm your cat."

I couldn't look at her face. Those perfectly white, perfectly aligned teeth of hers could blind an innocent bystander. Innocent, that was me all right. I'd *innocently* allowed her to care for Goofey. What an ignorant mistake.

"Please?" she begged. "Please forgive me, Holly?"

I wasn't ready to discuss this. The anger in me was too strong. So strong I couldn't even begin to put Matthew 5:44 into practice. "I can't talk now." I turned to find my jacket.

"Can I call you?" she pleaded.

"No." I stormed down the steps, feeling totally out of control as I waited for Stan in the foyer.

A few minutes later, the rest of the kids poured out of the chapel. Andie invited me to go with her to Denver in the morning to meet Christiana. "Dad wants to leave right after breakfast, around seven-thirty. Your mom can call the school and get an excused absence for you first thing tomorrow."

"Thanks for asking," I told her, only because I wanted to be with Andie.

Not because I wanted to meet Christiana. Not in the least.

♥ ♥ ♥

On the way to Denver, Andie and I sat in the backseat, singing last year's choir tour songs. When we ran out of songs, we played alliteration games, making sentences with words that started with the same letter.

I started. "Pathetic Paula parades her perfect pose, posture, and clothes. She pampers pets par excellence with pink poodle pajamas."

Andie chimed in. "Paula ponders Paris, posh parlors, and Park Avenue!"

"With palette paint on her cheeks and purple powder on her eyelids," I finished, giggling.

Mrs. Martinez turned around in her seat. "Girls, are you making fun of someone?"

Andie and I looked at each other. "Not really," Andie lied. We smothered giggles behind our hands.

All too soon, we arrived at the Denver International Airport. At least we had had two hours together before Christiana waltzed into our lives.

While Andie's dad parked the car, I looked at snapshots of Christiana. "Here's one," Andie said as we sat in the airport waiting area. "She's standing in front of Mozart's home in Salzburg. Can you imagine living in the same city as Mozart?"

"Bet you'd like to see it for yourself," I commented, studying the tall house with many windows.

Before she could answer, Andie's dad arrived, looking for the monitors posting departures and arrivals.

"There's one down there, Daddy," Andie said. We hurried to look at it.

"Let's see, flight 227 from New York . . . yep, it's on time." There was a certain amount of ecstasy in Andie's voice. I tried to overlook it. After all, this was a special moment for her.

Andie hurried to the archway that separates the arriving passengers from the baggage claim area. "I can't believe Christiana's almost here!"

I couldn't believe it, either. I was trying hard to squelch the green-eyed monster; it sure was causing me trouble.

Andie and I spotted the Austrian beauty right away. Being tall is an asset sometimes. She floated through the airport like some fairy-tale princess. A peaches-and-cream complexion graced her fair face, and she broke into a full smile at the sight of Andie. Hugging like long lost friends, the girls were lost in conversation. For what seemed like several minutes I waited, rather impatiently, for Andie to introduce me.

At long last, Andie turned to me. "Holly, I'd like you to meet Christiana Dertnig. And Christiana, this is a friend of mine, Holly Meredith."

Immediately my ears perked up. In just minutes I'd been reduced to a mere friend. What about lifelong *best* friend?

Christiana extended her hand. "So very nice

to meet you, Holly," she said. Perfect King's English.

I reached out, warming up my smile. "Same here," was all I could say.

"I've heard a lot about you from Andie's letters," Christiana said. "You're the girl Andie made up so you could fool your college pen pal, right?"

My face flamed. "Sort of," I mumbled. I disliked her instantly. Why'd she have to bring up one of the most embarrassing episodes of my life? And at our very first meeting!

Andie explained, "Christiana loves pulling tricks on people. They play jokes on each other all the time at her girls' school. She loved hearing about our plan to trick Lucas Leigh."

"That's nice," I said, fibbing through my teeth.

The entire trip home was spent discussing Christiana's hopes for her visit to America. One thing was clear: She wanted to attend a rock concert.

"Andie's never attended one," her mother said. "And I don't anticipate her father and I will change our minds about *that* issue."

Christiana's blue eyes widened. She was obviously shocked at the parental interference.

"There's a Mandee Trent concert in Denver next weekend," Andie's dad said. It was only a suggestion, but he seemed eager to steer the conversation away from rock concerts.

"Mandee Trent?" Christiana said. "Who's that?"

"She's a hot Christian pop singer," I volunteered.

"Oh," she said, like it was nothing.

"What about classical?" Andie's mother said. "I understand you enjoy Mozart."

Christiana the Great replied, "In Salzburg, we are surrounded by serious music."

"So maybe we should expose you to other types here," Andie said. She was beginning to sound like the Queen of England herself. I could hardly wait to get out of the car. Away from this strawberry blonde who seemed to affect everyone in her path.

Then Andie's mother mentioned my party. "Holly has a Valentine's Day birthday," she said. "And she's invited you both to a make-over party tonight."

Christiana had no idea what that was all about. Briefly, Andie explained.

I wasn't surprised when Christiana decided she would not be interested in a make-over. No doubt she was quite satisfied with her present look, thank you very much.

♥   ♥   ♥

That afternoon Andie escorted Christiana around to the principal and all the teachers at Dressel Hills Junior High. They'd been expecting her, of course, so the reception was red-carpet.

I ate lunch with Jared, without Andie. "Everyone's freaking out over Christiana," I moaned. "Especially Andie."

"It won't last forever," he assured me.

"Even Danny Myers is following her around, volunteering his services."

"Hmm," Jared said. "Sounds serious. Are you jealous?"

"Are you kidding?" I laughed, and Jared grinned. He knew Danny and I were ancient history. Jared was the only boy for me, even if he was a "dog" person.

All day I avoided Paula as best I could. And it wasn't easy. She kept showing up at the most conspicuous places. Places like the stall next to mine in the girls' bathroom. And in the exact same section of the library—three books down. This was turning into a nightmare. Mostly because I refused to forgive her. How many times had she asked—begged—for my pardon?

Seeing her grim face only reminded me of that horrible tube in my cat's stomach. Poor little Goofey. His suffering had been caused by a senseless act, and it was totally Paula's fault.

When it came to prayer, I avoided the forgiveness issue with God. It was much easier to pray about a zillion other things, like Goofey's restored health and Christiana's quick return to her homeland.

There was one request I asked for repeatedly, however. "Dear Lord," I prayed, curling up on my window seat after school. "I need your wisdom and help as fast as you can send it. It's about Goofey's next home. He needs a new one—fast! Please let it be a place where I can visit him every day. Could you do something soon? Amen."

I reached for my journal and recorded my thoughts.

Friday, February 11: I miss Andie already. Every time I looked for her at school today she was tied up with Christiana. I want to disappear and come back AFTER Christiana leaves!

The phone rang.

"Holly!" Mom called. "It's for you."

The vet was on the line. Goofey was being released tomorrow. A sad lump squeezed my throat.

"You'll need to monitor his eating and drinking for several more days," the vet reminded me.

I swallowed the lump. My heart was pounding. My darling Goofey was well, but for a cat without a home, this was horrible news. "Is there any way you can keep him a little longer?" I asked.

A short pause, then, "Is there a problem?"

Quickly, I shared my dilemma.

"We have a kennel of sorts," he explained, "but we can only keep him up to a week here."

"How much will it cost?" I thought of the birthday money I'd already started acquiring from relatives.

"About ten dollars a day," the vet said.

Mentally I tallied up my money. I had just enough to handle it. "Let's do that," I said. "Uh, only if I can visit Goofey every day."

"No problem. We'll look forward to seeing you. Good-bye."

I hung up the phone feeling a little better. But I wasn't independently wealthy, of course. And Mom must never find out about this. She wouldn't approve of using birthday money for Goofey's temporary housing.

When Stan arrived home, he took me for a quick visit with Goofey. My cat seemed much better, more energetic. And he licked my hand repeatedly as if to tell me so.

♥   ♥   ♥

When we returned home, I helped Mom set out the makeup and stuff for my birthday party. Together, we turned the kitchen into a beauty salon, complete with facial and beauty kits and hand mirrors for each girl. It was fabulous.

"The guests will be here in one hour," I said, thinking of the Patterson and Meredith family members. "Where are we gonna stash all our kids?"

"Well, let's see," Mom said, grinning. "Uncle Jack took Phil and Mark out for the evening. Stan's going to make himself scarce in his room, and Carrie and Stephie are planning their own party."

I sat down on a bar stool, absently picking up a creamy-pink blush. "I hope this make-over thing is a good idea." Christiana's snide remark this morning had me worried.

Mom stopped arranging things for a moment and looked at me. She pushed a stray hair off her forehead. "Is everything okay, Holly-Heart?"

"Not exactly," I said. "I really miss Andie."

I heard her sigh. Extra loud. "This isn't about Christiana, is it?"

"Who else?" I muttered.

I ran upstairs to change clothes. By the time I freshened up, slipped into a clean pair of jeans and sweater, Mom was knocking on my bedroom door.

I let her in.

"How's my birthday girl?"

"Oh, Mom." I ran into her outstretched arms. "I love you!"

She hugged me bone hard. "Let's start getting the sloppy joes ready. Your guests will be arriving very soon."

I followed her downstairs. It was amazing; Mom could calm me down, no matter what. One of her many God-given gifts.

Speaking of gifts, Daddy sent me money from California, as usual. I wondered what my best friend would give me for my fourteenth birthday. As for Christiana, I would be lucky if she cracked her face to give me the slightest smile.

The doorbell rang; I ran to get it. Shauna and Joy were first to arrive. A few minutes later Amy-Liz showed up. By the time I'd hung up their jackets, the doorbell rang again. This time it was Andie with her shadow—er, pen pal—Christiana.

"Happy birthday," Andie said, giving me a big hug.

"Thanks," I said. "Glad you're here."

Christiana reached out to shake my hand like she had at the airport this morning. Reluctantly, I held out mine.

Z-z-z-z-t-t! I shrieked and jumped back. Christiana had zapped me with a hand zinger.

"Ooh, she got you good, Holly," Amy-Liz exclaimed. The girls laughed.

"Are you all right?" Christiana said, trying not to smirk.

I nodded, forcing a smile.

Andie giggled. "Remember, I told you Christiana loves practical jokes."

Rubbing the zing off my palm, I led them into the kitchen. Christiana immediately launched off on entertaining my guests with her stories. She talked about Vienna and Mozart's *The Magic Flute*. I couldn't imagine Amy-Liz or Shauna or any of the others being half as interested as they looked. I was the one interested in classical music. They were die-hard Mandee Trent fans.

"What's school like in Salzburg?" I asked.

"I attend a boarding school," Christiana said. "It's an all-girl school."

"You sleep over?" Amy-Liz asked.

Christiana chuckled. "It's great fun. We pull jokes on each other nearly every night."

I'll bet you do, I thought.

"Tell us some tricks you've played," Amy-Liz said.

"I'm sure you've heard of the hand-in-warm-water trick," Christiana said.

Everyone nodded, laughing.

"And there's the greased toilet seat," she said.

"We did that last year on choir tour," Andie piped up, glancing at me.

Christiana was all too eager to go on. And on.

Leaning against the kitchen bar, I decided it was time to divert the conversation away from Christiana's neck of the woods. "Did you hear?

Mandee Trent's coming to Denver—one week from tonight."

"I already bought my ticket," Joy said.

"Me too," Shauna said.

"She sings like an angel," Amy-Liz said.

Andie spoke. "I heard she's dating some guy in her band."

Amy-Liz stood up and sauntered around, pretending to play the sax. "Wouldn't it be cool to travel together all over the country?"

"How romantic," I said, keeping my eyes on Christiana.

"What sort of professional training does she have?" Miss Austria asked, tilting her head.

I wanted to say, *Who needs training when you can sing like an angel?* but I stifled my thoughts and watched the reactions of the others.

Andie described Miss Trent's vocal training to a T. For Christiana's sake. As always.

Mom saved the day by announcing supper. We gathered around the dining room table where brightly colored name cards decorated each place setting. I spotted Andie's name beside Christiana's. Even my own mother was watching out for Christiana. Not for me.

Soon we were seated. "Let's pray," Mom said, and she began. First a special blessing on the birthday girl, then a joyful thanks to the Lord for "Holly's friends, each one of them," and last a food blessing. Everyone joined in with "amen" at the end. All but Christiana.

"Andie, start the buns and the chips around," I said.

Mom took the girls' soda orders and left the room while Andie began describing sloppy joes in great detail to Christiana. When she finished with the ingredients, she said, "My mom makes them every Monday night."

"Sometimes my mother sneaks leftovers in the hamburger mix," Amy-Liz complained. "It's disgusting."

"That's nothing," Joy said. "My mom uses ground turkey for our sloppy joes."

"Eeew!" the girls squealed.

After supper, Mom brought out the cake. The girls sang the birthday song while I contemplated my wish. Birthday wishes are supposed to be special. Very special.

Mom lit the candles. "Happy birthday, Holly-Heart."

I closed my eyes, wishing for the day when I would be number one again with Andie. Taking a deep breath, I blew out my candles. All but one.

"Don't worry, Holly," Andie said, eyeing the lone candle. "Today's not your real birthday, is it?"

I didn't know how to take her remark. I

hoped she was being kind. But she sounded a bit catty. Anyway, my wish would never come true now. Thanks to one lousy candle.

For the gift opening, we converged on the living room and sat on the floor. I observed Christiana, noticing her shining eyes as she glanced at my gifts lined up on the sofa. She held hers tightly, fingering the pink bow in the center. Did she think her gift was more wonderful than all the rest?

I opened hers last, and soon discovered it was from both her *and* Andie. The gift was a jewelry box, which meant it probably wasn't Andie's idea at all. And by the sound of the Mozart tune, I was sure Christiana had chosen it.

To make things worse, when the beautician showed up, Christiana suddenly developed a headache. Andie turned on her friendly charm and arranged for her mom to pick them up.

"Why can't you stay?" I cornered Andie, pleading with her.

"It's Christiana's first day here, and I'm her host," she reminded me rather coldly. "She probably has jet lag. It's two o'clock in the morning in Austria right now, you know." And with that comment, she flounced off to get their jackets.

We started the facials without them. Andie and Christiana sat in the living room, whispering and giggling while they waited for their ride. I sat in the kitchen with the rest of the girls while Joy smeared Andie's cucumber mask on my face. After it dried, I cracked it twice on purpose thinking about Christiana. She had to be so perfect. Every word, every gesture . . .

It was so disgusting. Besides that, she had Andie wrapped around her little finger.

Could my friendship with Andie survive five more weeks of this freak show?

When Andie's mother arrived, I was polite. I thanked the girls for the birthday present and said good-bye. But in my heart I was crushed.

Passing through the dining room, I saw it: a huge black spider hidden in the crevice of a chair. I froze. I'd sat in that very spot tonight!

Inching my way past it, I gulped. Then I ran to the kitchen to get a broom.

"What's that for?" Joy asked, eyeing me suspiciously.

"Don't worry," I said. "Stay right where you are."

That brought all the girls running.

"Don't anybody move," I said as they huddled behind me, squealing. Bam! I came down hard on the monstrous insect. The girls leaned in, staring—holding their mouths.

"It's not dead!" Amy-Liz cried.

"Whack it again," Shauna screamed.

I raised the broom over my head, preparing for the kill.

"What kind of spider is it?" Joy asked.

"Indestructible," Amy-Liz said.

With broom poised, I inched closer, poking the spider with the wooden handle. The ugly creature didn't move.

"It's fake," I said.

That rotten girl, I thought of Christiana.

"Hey, good joke," Amy-Liz said. Joy and Shauna agreed.

I snatched up the lifelike critter and flung it at them. Screams filled the house, and Mom came running.

"It's nothing," I said. But it was. Christiana had arrived only a few hours ago, and already she was messing up my life. Stealing the show at my party. Stealing my best friend . . .

Back in the kitchen, I checked my facial mask in one of the hand mirrors lying on the counter. An alien-green tint covered my face. Cucumber facial masks are supposed to look like that. But I got carried away and imagined that my eyes were green as emeralds, too. *Green with envy*, I thought. *Look at me! I'm just a green-eyed monster*. But I didn't care.

Amy-Liz got brave and had her curly blond hair cut and styled. Joy and Shauna liked it so much they experimented with a new look, too.

Even without Andie, the make-over went pretty well. We made shy, sweet Joy look like a flirt with bright red, wet lipstick and tons of mascara. Shauna was grotesque with whitened lips, dark eye shadow, and dark eyebrows. Amy-Liz went for the clown look with round circles of rouge on each cheek and on the tip of her nose. I wasn't much of a sport and did the natural look. The real me—nothing new.

When the girls left for home, I helped Mom clean up.

"You didn't have much fun tonight," she said, wiping the kitchen counters.

"It was fun, I just . . ." What could I say? Turning fourteen wasn't what it was cracked up to be. "I don't know," I said, twisting the lids on the foundation and cream blush. "Maybe it's just when you look forward to something so long, you have a mental image of how it'll turn out. Then when Christiana started telling her boring stories, I felt icky inside."

"I understand, honey." She gathered up the dirty napkins.

"Then Christiana got sick, which I seriously doubt, and Andie left, too." It was hard recounting the miserable evening. I didn't want to think about it. Writing my feelings secretly in my journal was much easier.

So I kissed Mom on the cheek and wiped my tears. "I'll be upstairs for a while," I said. "Thanks for everything."

February 11 continued: The party was weird. It was mostly a welcoming party for Christiana! Ick!

Goofey goes in the kennel tomorrow. Poor thing. I'll be broke by the end of the week. But I'll use all my allowance next month for my missionary project and the sponsor child for sure.

A strange sensation rippled through my scalp, down my shoulders, and into my spine. I shivered and stopped writing. It felt like someone was reading over my shoulder.

Slowly looking up, I half expected to see an angel, or . . . maybe God himself. But then, why would God need to read my words when He already knew them?

At that moment, Bearie-O fell off the shelf, landing in my lap. I stroked the top of his bald teddy head. The loving had worn it thin.

Bearie-O was symbolic of my friendship with Andie. Thinking back on the amazing bond we shared, I felt myself becoming even more jealous of Andie's attention to Christiana. I grabbed my journal and counted out the days. Thirty-four to go! March 17, St. Patrick's Day, was the day Christiana was scheduled to leave. I drew a giant smiley face over the date and wrote in big letters: CHRISTIANA GO HOME!

♥   ♥   ♥

Valentine's Day, my true birthday, came at last. A giant red envelope was stuck to my locker at school. I spotted it as I pushed through the crowded hallway.

"Happy Valentine birthday," Jared whispered in my ear as I reached for his card.

I grinned back at him. "Thanks," I said. "Is it for Valentine's or my birthday?"

"Look inside," he said slyly.

I tore the envelope open. A card with red and pink hearts wished me a Happy Valentine's Day. The card behind it was homemade. Light pink construction paper, folded in quarters with pen and ink designs around the edges. The verse was without rhyme—free verse.

"This is incredible!" I said, referring to the homemade card and verse. "You're good, Jared. Thanks!"

"Thank you, m'lady . . . for being born, that is." He was bowing and flirting like no other, and it was fabulous.

I opened my locker, hiding my blushing face.

"Happy birthday!" I heard an all too familiar voice. Andie's. But I kept my face inside my locker.

Jared leaned next to me. "You're being paged."

"Is she with Christiana?" I muttered.

"Who else?" he teased.

Both girls came right up to my locker. "You look the same," Andie commented. "Thought you were having a make-over."

I dragged up a smile.

Jared saved the day. "You girls going to hear Mandee Trent Friday night?"

Andie pulled something out of her jeans pocket. "Two tickets say we'll be there." She held them up.

Christiana smiled—at Jared. "I am dying to see what everyone is talking about," she chimed in, using one of Andie's expressions.

"I guarantee you'll enjoy yourself," Jared said. "The church is taking a busload to Denver."

Without missing a beat, Christiana said, "Oh, save us some seats, will you, Jared?" She flashed him a dazzling smile.

"Absolutely," Jared said.

I felt uneasy. He seemed just a little too friendly with the Austrian beauty.

♥ ♥ ♥

Later, Jared met me at lunch. "What's going

on with you and Andie?" he asked, sliding in beside me at the table.

"I don't want to talk about it." I watched Andie and Christiana out of the corner of my eye.

"This doesn't have anything to do with Christiana, does it?" He was prying, and I didn't like it.

"Let's just say I'm sick of hearing about the Alps and Mozart's birthplace and fakey headaches."

Jared frowned. "Headaches?"

I told him about my birthday party and Christiana's sudden illness.

"What's so bad about an impromptu headache?" He grinned at me.

I sighed. "Maybe if you'd been there . . ."

Jared reached for my hand. "You're jealous," he said casually.

I sprinkled hot sauce on my tacos. "You could say that."

"It doesn't become you, Holly."

"Don't preach. You'll start sounding like Danny."

"I don't care who I sound like," he said. "Christiana probably isn't a Christian. At least, I get that impression."

"Well, if you're so interested, why don't you convert her?" I didn't mean to sound so harsh; it just tumbled out. Maybe because Andie and Christiana were heading toward our table right then. "Excuse me," I said, hopping up.

"Hey, where're you going?" Jared leaped up, leaving his tray behind.

"Enjoy your lunch. And your company."

But Jared followed me down the hall to my locker. He stared at me while I worked my combination lock. "Don't mess up your birthday, Holly-Heart," he said softly.

"Then don't bug me about Andie. She's *my* problem."

He ran his fingers through his hair. "If that's the way you want it."

Looking at his face, I felt lousy. Jared accepted me as I was, guilty or not guilty. He was only trying to help smooth things over with Andie. After all, it wasn't the first time she and I had fought.

"Hey, you're riding to Denver with me on the bus," he said, changing the subject. "Okay?"

I groaned. "I would, but my family's going skiing, and I just—"

"Just want to stay away from Andie," he interrupted.

"Skiing's a good excuse, don't you think?" I said, avoiding his eyes.

"But it won't be half as much fun without you."

"I'm sorry." I really was.

"I know."

That was another thing I liked about Jared. He wasn't pushy. He accepted things the way they were. For now, our friendship was comfortable, secure. Had Andie filled Christiana in on Jared and me?

I headed for PE. Andie and her sidekick would be there, sharing the same gym locker. It was hopeless the way Christiana finagled everything to her benefit. Why couldn't Andie see the light?

12

Timed tests were scheduled for the last half of PE. And wouldn't you know it, Christiana and I were competing for first place. On ropes, no less!

Shaking uncontrollably, every muscle in my body straining with each pull, I did my best to block Christiana from my view. It was impossible. Her strawberry blond hair swayed as she slithered up the rope with her long, slender legs. Closing my eyes, I inched upward. Finally I reached the top.

The class was cheering . . . screaming. I'd made it! Opening my eyes, I saw the girls gathered around Christiana like she was a celebrity or something. Her smile of victory made me ill. I was wrong. She'd beat me hands down.

Sliding down slowly, I noticed Paula was waiting at the bottom of the rope.

"You almost tied her." She flashed her toothpaste smile.

I ignored her.

Andie was next for the test. I felt sick inside, helplessly watching her hang in midair, unable to get her chubby legs to assist in the climb. She barely made it to the first mark. Whew, that hurt.

I couldn't watch anymore.

Miss Tucker kept me after class. She said encouraging things about my rope time, but I still felt resentment toward Christiana. "You're good, Meredith," Miss Tucker said. "I'd like to see you get more athletically involved around here."

"Thanks." I glanced at the wall clock. She'd kept me too long. I had to hit the showers fast.

She patted me on the shoulder. "I hear you're having a birthday today. Hope it's a good one."

"Thanks." I headed for the steps to the locker room.

Paula was waiting. "How's Goofey?" she asked.

This girl never quits, I thought, mustering up two words. "Goofey's better." Of course, I avoided the kennel issue entirely.

"We can't be late for the math test," Paula said as we hurried downstairs.

I unlocked my gym locker and pulled out my clothes and a clean towel. Andie and Christiana were already dressing for class. I was really late.

"Is Goofey having visitors yet?" Paula persisted.

I was sick of the questions. "Only me."

"Well, I hope you have a happy birthday, Holly," she said, closing her gym locker.

"Yeah, right," I muttered as I undressed.

I stuffed my sweaty gym clothes into my locker, wrapped my towel around me, and headed for the showers, leaving my locker open. Time was running out. Our math teacher was a stickler for being prompt. Her pet peeve was kids who showed up late for class. She was known to knock a whole letter grade off a test for every five minutes a student was late.

I hurried into the shower room. Piling up my jeans, sweater, and clean underwear next to the wall near the shower, I hopped in.

Soaping up quickly, I relived Christiana's look of triumph when she had beat me on the ropes.

Poor Andie, short and chubby—what a nightmare the ropes had always been for her. If Christiana cared about Andie's feelings at all, she'd have been cheering her on instead of gloating about winning first place.

"Holly, hurry!" It was Paula. "We have five minutes to get to math," she hollered.

Peeking out of the shower stall, I saw Paula applying mascara with one hand while holding a compact with the other. Her hair was still damp from her shower. Could I never escape this girl?

Careful not to get my own hair too wet, I rinsed off quickly. Then, reaching for my towel, I dried off in record speed. Funny, it wasn't Andie reminding me about math. She was probably in class already, choosing a seat next to the Austrian Olympian.

I wrapped my damp towel around me and reached for my clothes. But the spot where I'd put them was empty. "That's strange," I said. Someone had moved my clothes by mistake.

Tiptoeing out of the shower, I looked around. My feet grew colder with each step on the wet cement floor. Scrambling over the full length of the room, I was frustrated. "I know I put them right here," I said out loud.

Wait a minute. Paula was just here, I thought. *What was she still doing here?*

That's when I saw the note. Leaning over, I picked it up. Someone had written: HAPPY "BIRTHDAY SUIT" in purple ink on the paper.

Was it Paula? I gripped the note and the corners of my towel. The clamor of the next class added to my confusion as they came bustling into the locker room.

I clumped toward my locker.

"You're late, Meredith," Miss Tucker yelled over the locker room noise.

"My clothes are gone," I said, but she was too busy to pay attention. Flinging my gym locker wide open, I looked inside. It was empty!

Where were my things? How would I ever make it to math?

Still clasping the note, I retraced my steps to the shower stalls, frantic to find my clothes. Where would a prankster hide them? In desperation, I choked the tears back. Wiping my eyes, I examined the handwriting on the note once again. I didn't recognize it. And, of course, it wasn't signed.

Clutching the note and the towel, I darted back into the locker area. I gazed up at the clock. Two o'clock. The math test was starting now.

Dizzy with rage, I stumbled to my open locker, pushed the note inside, and slammed the door.

"Holly!"

I spun around. It was Paula.

"What do you want?" I gripped the towel.

"I saw what she did."

"Who?"

"Christiana. She took your things and ran off before I could catch her. I even followed her to math class, but I didn't want to make a scene, so I came back to help you." She turned to open her locker and began to undress.

I stared at her. "What are you doing?"

"I'll wear my gym clothes to class. I always keep a clean pair in here just in case," she explained, tossing her sweater to me.

"I can't take your clothes," I muttered, dumbfounded.

"Why not?" she said, throwing her jeans at me. "That's what friends are for."

She slipped into some blue sweats and pulled a T-shirt over her head. "You can still make it if you hurry," she said as she fluffed her brunette locks and ran out of the locker room.

I was speechless.

After school, Jared caught up with me at the bus stop. He whipped out a birthday present with a flourish. "Ta-dah!" he announced. "Okay if I ride with the cutest girl in Dressel Hills?"

"Sure," I said, forcing a happy face as I pulled my jacket tight against me. Jared had noticed I was wearing different clothes. I could tell by the way he looked at me. After all, I didn't exactly fill out Paula Miller's clothes the way she did. But it was better than the "birthday suit" by far!

Out of the corner of my eye I noticed Andie and Christiana coming, half a block away. They were walking fast at first, but I was sure they'd spotted me because suddenly they slowed their pace. I kept my eyes on Jared, refusing to acknowledge their presence.

I vowed right there to begin the silent treatment. It was the ultimate punishment for their sin. Not that Andie had done anything wrong, but wasn't it her fault Miss Austria was here in the first place?

On the bus, Jared slid into the seat beside me. "Open your gift, Holly-Heart."

I gasped when I saw the CD—Mandee Trent's latest release. "I love it," I said. "Thanks, Jared."

"You're welcome." He winked at me.

"This is so cool. Now I can ski with Mandee Trent coming through my Discman while you watch her hit the stage in Denver." Such a romantic thought.

"Shall we synchronize the moment?" he asked.

I poked him. "Don't be silly," I teased, but secretly I loved the idea of listening to my new CD at the exact same moment as Jared was experiencing the live performance. He reached for my hand and held it. *Fabulous*.

Downhill Court came up all too quickly. I thanked Jared again for the CD before getting off the bus.

"See you tomorrow," he called.

"Bye!" I held the gift close as I hurried across the snow-packed street.

Once in the privacy of my bedroom, I let my anger pour out in the safest place of all: my journal. First I recorded my intentions for the vow of silence. I would refuse to speak to Andie until she apologized. No, better yet, until she literally *pleaded* with me to return as her number one best friend.

Next I removed Paula's clothes and tossed them in the hamper. What a remarkable thing she had done today. Something *I* might have done for a best friend.

Slipping into my robe, I popped my new CD into the player on my desk. Mandee Trent's voice wafted through the air. Perfect. I pulled a mystery novel off the shelf and curled up on my window seat, trying to forget the events of the day.

The harsh reality of my plan hit me hard when the phone rang. "For you, Holly," Carrie called to me from the hallway. "It's Andie."

"Tell her I'm not here," I said. Abandoning my book, I jumped up and headed for the stairs. "It's the truth . . . I'm not here." I raced down the steps, through the kitchen, and out the back door.

It was sub-zero cold out there and I counted, slowly, to thirty-five, shivering in my robe as I waited for Carrie to tell me she was off the phone.

But she never did, and I stumbled back into the kitchen, freezing half to death. "Carrie," I called to her.

Stephie, not Carrie, came running up the steps from the family room. "Carrie can't talk now, she's not here," she mimicked me, straight-faced. Then she burst into giggles.

"Get out," I said, chasing after her.

I found Carrie doing her homework. "What did she want?" I asked.

Carrie looked up, eyes filled with innocence. "Who?"

"You said Andie called." I leaned over the back of the sectional staring into her pixie face. "What did she say?"

"She said you're a goof brain."

I couldn't believe this. "You are so not cool." I left the room in a huff.

♥   ♥   ♥

Wednesday after school Stan drove me to visit my cat. "How do you feel about missing the Mandee Trent concert?" I asked as we waited for a red light.

"I don't have to see her on stage. Besides, it'll be great skiing." He looked both ways before entering the intersection.

"What does Andie think about it?"

"No big deal," he said. "Andie's got Christiana. They'll have a good time together."

"You're right," I said. "Christiana the clothes crook."

He frowned. "Huh?"

I told him the horrible thing Christiana had done after gym class.

"I can't imagine Andie letting Christiana do that," Stan said. "Doesn't sound like her."

"No kidding."

He dropped me off in front of the animal clinic. "I'll be back in thirty minutes," he said.

It was fabulous spending time with Goofey. He actually smiled when he saw me, the way he always did—before Paula tried to poison him.

"I've been praying about a home for you," I whispered to him. "God must have something very special planned. He just hasn't let me know yet."

Goofey purred contentedly as if to say: Whatever you can do is fine, thank you.

"One day at a time," I said softly in his ear.

But deep inside, I was worried. Who in Dressel Hills could I convince to adopt my adorable cat? True, he wasn't the prettiest cat around. But beauty comes from within, after all.

Stan beeped his horn. I kissed Goofey goodbye and headed outside into the cold mountain air.

♥　♥　♥

At home, Carrie was waiting. Her bright eyes danced with delirious delight as she informed me of the numerous phone calls I'd missed. From guess who.

"Andie's dying to talk to you, Holly," Carrie said. "It's gotta be important."

"Yeah, well, that's too bad," I retorted, sticking by my vow.

"If she were my best friend, I'd at least ask my sister to take a message." Carrie's eyes danced with mischief.

"Look," I said, sitting her down. "Andie's not your best friend, and you can forget about lecturing me. Okay?"

"Mommy!" Carrie shouted, running out of the room.

"Fine, go tell Mom," I muttered, disappearing into my room. I slammed the door shut.

Settling on my window seat, I grabbed two pillows and leaned against the wall. The sun's rays made me drowsy as I relived the birthday-suit nightmare. . . .

I was in the shower again. At school. Reaching for a towel, I searched for my clothes.

"Put your clothes on," one seventh grader called.

The girls began to laugh. Echoing into a mighty roar, the laughter hurt my head, my ears. I cupped my hands over them, forgetting about the towel. It slipped away as I ran, naked, up the stairs.

At the top of the steps, I hid behind the door. I could see the math classroom just across the outside courtyard.

It was snowy and cold out there. I cringed. And then I saw her—Andie—my best friend in the world. She was waving something at me across the courtyard. "Hurry, Holly," she called. "You can still make it!"

I struggled to see what she had in her hands. Squinting, I peered through the snowy brightness. Then, for a moment, she stopped waving and I could see clearly.

My clothes! Andie had my clothes.

Whoosh! A blast of arctic air ripped through the courtyard, snatching them out of her hands. They flew at me, icy and hostile, sticking to my body. Covering me with their freezing, unfriendly fabric.

I looked down at the expensive clothes stuck to me. Labels and brand names I'd never heard of leaped up. M.A.D. Collection, Angry Jeans Co., and Bonjealous. I tried desperately to remove the tags, but my fingers were frozen.

Again, I struggled, clawing at the hideous labels. Anger . . . jealousy . . .

"Holly-Heart, wake up!"

I opened my eyes. "W-wha-at?" I mumbled,

still half asleep. "Where am I?"

"You're right here in your room, darling," Mom said, kissing my head.

I looked down. The tags on two throw pillows were pulled off. One of the heart-shaped ones had a hole in its seam.

My fingers must've gone to sleep. I let the pillows roll onto the window seat as I made a fist with both hands, limbering up my tingling fingers, still numb from the dream.

"You missed a long-distance call," Mom said, a hint of a smile playing around her lips.

"I did?" I yawned.

"It was Tyler, your stepbrother." She sat down beside me on my window seat, holding a cup of tea.

"Tyler? Oh yeah. In California."

"He asked when he should call again."

I stood up, stretching my legs. "What did you say?"

"That you'd be expecting his call around four-thirty our time."

I hugged her. "Why didn't you wake me?"

"You looked so peaceful in here, I just couldn't."

"But I was having a nightmare!"

"Well, you looked peaceful," she said, sipping her tea. "Are you anxious to go skiing?"

"What about you? It's your first time, Mom. Aren't you scared?"

"Oh, but Jack will be there," Mom said, a flush of color dancing in her cheeks. "He'll teach me just fine." And by that, I knew the honeymoon was still going strong.

When Mom left the room, I shivered, thinking about those horrible labels stuck on me. I couldn't get it out of my mind. Deep inside, I was still trying to rip the labels off my clothes.

Thank goodness it was only a dream.

14

At four-thirty the phone rang.

"I'll get it!" yelled Carrie.

"I've got it!" shouted Stan.

"It's for me," I said.

Three of us picked up the phones in the house. Tyler was calling from California.

"Hey, Tyler," Carrie said.

Click. Stan hung up.

"How's California?" I asked.

"Fine, thanks," he said. "Happy birthday, Holly . . . a little late. Wait'll you see what I bought you. It's way cool!"

I laughed. "Give me a hint."

"Nope, you just wait. My mom's mailing it today."

"Is it nice there?" I asked.

"About seventy-five degrees, I think. Here, ask Sean, he's baby-sitting me."

Sean? My heart pounded. Why did *he* want to talk to me?

"Hang up the phone," I said to Carrie.

"Why?" she whined.

"Just do it!"

Before I could say any more to her, Sean was on the line. "Hey, Holly. How was your birthday?"

I'd forgotten how deep his voice was. "Don't ask," I said, laughing. No way was I telling him about the birthday-suit prank. "What's it like there?"

"It's great, as always, but I'm ready for a change."

Click. Carrie hung up. Boring weather talk does it every time.

"Your dad's thinking of coming to Denver on business next month," Sean continued. "If things work out, he'll bring Tyler and me along to ski." He paused. "Uh, I'd like to see you if we come to Dressel Hills."

Was this for real?

"You're coming here?"

"Over spring break," he volunteered. "It's the busiest time of the season, but school's out. Your dad thought it would be perfect timing."

I was suddenly shy again, like when I'd first met him on the beach last Christmas. "Sounds fun," I said. "Carrie will be thrilled to see Tyler again. They were quite a pair last Christmas."

"Well, I better let you go, Holly. But I'd like to write you a letter, if it's okay."

"Uh, sure," I said.

"Nice talking to you. Bye."

"Bye," I said, still shocked at his news. Coming to Dressel Hills? Next month?

I hung up the phone and ran to tell Carrie. Then I stopped cold. What was I thinking? She would blab this to everyone. The whole town would know about Sean Hamilton, the cute California surfer.

I decided not to record my conversation with Sean in my journal, either. Too risky. Especially with Andie teaming up with Christiana to do horrible things to me these days.

Somehow I kept things quiet about Sean through supper. And Carrie never even asked why I wanted to talk to him alone on the phone.

❤   ❤   ❤

On Thursday Paula cornered me in the hall after school. Kayla was waiting for her several feet away. I noticed Paula's designer jeans and her new denim jacket. She looked completely different from her twin.

She probably wants her clothes back, I thought.

"How's Goofey?" asked Paula.

"Better."

"I'd love to see him again," she said, shifting her books from one arm to the other.

"I, uh, don't know," I stuttered. No way did I want to share my precious time with Goofey. Not with the cat killer.

Around the corner came Andie and Christiana, laughing and talking. No doubt they were staying after school again. Together.

"Hey," Andie said, smiling at me.

"Hey," Paula replied, wearing a flashy smile. "How are you doing on your science project?"

"It's almost finished," Andie told Paula. Then she looked at me. Almost sadly. "How's *your* project, Holly?"

Christiana butted in. "Andie and I are doing a joint project, you know." She was playing her "one-up" game again. And she didn't have to remind me. Andie and I had planned to do the project together. Before Christiana came and spoiled everything.

She continued her chatter. Several times, Andie made attempts to talk to me, but Miss Austria monopolized the conversation. I didn't care . . . the silent treatment was still in force.

I excused myself, turned, and walked away.

When I was out of their sight, I fled from the building.

Paula caught up with me at the bus stop. "Holly, wait! I have to talk to you," she sputtered, out of breath.

"Forget it. I don't want to hear anything about *her*," I snapped, referring to Andie.

"You have to," she insisted. "It's a matter of . . ." She stopped.

"What? Life and death?" I climbed onto the bus and pushed my way as far back as possible.

Paula followed me. "Please listen, Holly." Her eyes pleaded with me, serious concern written on her face.

Struggling with my curiosity and the vow of silence, I clunked my backpack on the floor and folded my arms across my chest.

"May I sit here?" she persisted.

"I need to be alone."

"But—"

"I *need* to be alone," I said.

A sad, lonely expression swept across her face. Hesitating, she turned away, searching for a seat. At last she chose the only other one available on the entire bus—beside her twin.

Torn between missing Andie and hating her, I dug around inside my backpack, looking for my mystery novel. Finding it, I opened to the bookmark and began to read as the bus made its lurching stops and starts.

Halfway down the page I glanced up, staring at Paula. *What was the message from Andie?*

I forced my attention away from her so-called important info, reading a few more pages in my book. Then the bus stopped in front of the doughnut shop and a bunch of kids got off, dashing inside to claim the "Sweet of the Day."

Kayla crawled over Paula to get out, expecting her to come along. But Paula shook her head and stayed, gazing out the window as the bus doors whooshed shut.

I couldn't help watching her as the bus made its journey down the long stretch on Aspen Street toward Downhill Court.

♥ ♥ ♥

Carrie met me as I came in the house. "Bad news," she announced, closing the front door behind me.

"The worst," Stephie added, sitting on a chair with her feet tucked under her.

"Now what?" I plopped my backpack on the sofa.

"We're staying home. The ski trip's off," Carrie moaned.

"You're kidding." I pulled my jacket off.

"Would I joke about this?" she whined.

I hung up my jacket. "So what's going on?" I noticed Mom's coat was missing from the closet. "Where's Mom?"

"She's at Uncle Jack's office," Carrie said, looking serious. "They got real busy."

"Yeah," Stephie said. "Looks like we're stuck at home." She shrugged.

"Are you sure? We're *not* going skiing?"

I went into the kitchen to hide my delight. Hurrying to the phone, I called Amy-Liz, telling her the news. It looked like I was going to the Mandee Trent concert after all!

"This is so cool, Holly," Amy-Liz said. "But you'd better hurry and get your ticket."

Just then, Stan burst through the back door. I waved at him, trying to get his attention. "Uh, I'll have to talk to you later," I told Amy-Liz, hanging up.

"Didja hear?" Stan said, his nose in the fridge.

"I know, the ski trip is off," I said. "Who told you?"

"I ran into Dad downtown after school. Something's come up with his business. It's booming." Stan poured a glass of milk. "But we're going for sure next weekend."

Oh no! I thought. *That's when Andie and*

Christiana are going skiing. I slumped onto the chair in the corner beside Mom's desk.

"What's the matter with you?" he asked.

"Nothing much." I pushed away thoughts of bumping into Andie on the slopes.

"Here, go get yourself a ticket." He shelled out thirty-five bucks. "That oughta help you smile again, little sister." It was John Wayne again.

"Hey, what happened to your birthday stash?" Carrie demanded.

I glared at her. No way could she know my money was going for Goofey's room and board. She wouldn't hesitate to tattle to Mom about it. I had enough problems without that, too.

"Are you broke?" Carrie asked.

I waved her off. "I just made an investment." I grinned my thanks to Stan, who grabbed a bag of potato chips and sat down at the bar. "Are you going to the concert?"

"Nah," he said. "I've got an appointment."

"Andie won't like it when she finds out," I said, sliding onto a bar stool across from him.

"Aw, she'll get over it," he said, pulling a John Wayne video out of his pocket. I wished I could approach my relationship with Andie the way Stan did.

Eager to order a ticket, I picked up the portable phone. First one recorded message then another came on the line as I followed the directions, pushing the correct numbers for additional information. Finally an actual person answered.

"I'd like to reserve one ticket for the concert at McNichols Arena in Denver tomorrow night," I said, twitching with delight. Jared would be *so* excited.

"One moment, please," the woman said as recorded music greeted my ear.

I waited, visualizing the trip up and back on the church bus. It would be so fabulous. Jared would probably hold my hand. . . .

"Miss?" came the voice.

"Yes?"

"That performance is sold out," she said coldly.

My heart sank. "Thank you," I said as a wave of disappointment descended over my heart.

I hung up the phone.

No tickets? Not a single one?

If Andie and I had been on speaking terms, I would have called her right then and cried on her shoulder. But no, she was busy doing her joint project with Christiana. Besides, it wasn't time for me to break my vow of silence.

Dejected and alone, I trudged downstairs and returned Stan's money. His eyes and attention were focused on his latest John Wayne video. He stuffed the money back into his wallet without saying a word.

It made me think of my missions project. I was eager to send the money, but I'd have to wait till Goofey was settled in a new home.

I shuddered at the thought. Heading for the kitchen, I heard the phone ring.

Carrie got it. She stuffed another cookie in

her mouth. "Iths fer you."

"Who is it?"

She shrugged.

I took the phone from her sticky fingers. "Hello?"

"Holly?"

It was Paula.

"I can't talk now," I said and hung up.

"How rude," Carrie said, sliding off her stool.

"Just stay out of this."

The phone rang again. I let it ring and ring. At last, it stopped.

"Brat," I said.

"I'm telling Mom," she hollered.

"Fine." I headed for a sink full of dirty dishes.

Carrie stomped off. "I'll be in my room, and I'm not coming out as long as you live in this house!"

"Perfect."

Stacking the dishes in the dishwasher, I thought about Paula. Why was she calling? Was the message from Andie *that* important?

Stan called from the family room. "Dad just phoned. They're on their way home. He said to take some meat out to thaw for supper."

I hurried to the freezer, thinking of the bone-thin child on the church bulletin board. Was it right for me to spend money to keep Goofey in the kennel when there were kids starving to death in the world?

♥ ♥ ♥

I debated about staying in bed all day when Mom knocked on my door the next morning. "It's a beautiful day in the Rockies," she sang.

Groaning, I rolled over. Everyone in the world was going to hear Mandee Trent tonight. Everyone except me. I dragged myself out of bed and stared at my face in the mirror.

Hopeless.

Mom peeked her head into the room again. "Holly-Heart," she said, "let's plan to go shopping, maybe next week after school?"

I knew what she meant. Mom and I always went shopping after I'd accumulated birthday money from relatives in Pennsylvania and California.

I shrugged my shoulders. It was time to divulge my secret. I'd kept it from her too long.

"My birthday money's gone," I admitted, spilling out the whole story of Goofey's whereabouts.

Mom's mouth dropped open. "You used your money on a cat?"

I nodded ruefully, bracing myself for the lecture.

But she just sighed and said, "Well, it's your money. I guess you should spend it the way you want to." She frowned a bit, though.

Nothing more was said about Goofey, so I told her my plans for next month's allowance. "I want to sponsor at least one starving child," I announced, "and one of the missionaries on the bulletin board at church."

"But you shouldn't be giving away all your money," Mom said gently. "You need some of it to do things with your friends and family. And don't forget you need to start saving for college, too."

"I know," I said. "But I want to do something for other people, too."

Mom pulled me close. "You're all heart," she whispered.

Mom left, and I got dressed for the day. I felt better . . . at least about telling Mom where I'd spent my birthday money. But I kept thinking about the Mandee Trent concert I was going to miss. Nothing could make me feel better about *that*.

The phone rang during breakfast. Uncle Jack licked waffle syrup off his fingers and reached for the portable phone. "Meredith-Patterson residence. Jack speaking."

A short pause, then . . . "Holly, it's for you. Paula Miller's on the line." He passed the phone to me.

Carrie snickered at me across the table. She knew there was no way I'd hang up now. Not on Uncle Jack's business partner's daughter.

I took a deep breath. "Hello?"

"Please don't be mad, Holly," she began. "I had to call you early. Just listen—"

I interrupted, pretending to answer her. "Okay, I'll see you at school."

"But, Holly—"

"I have to go now," I said. *Politely.* For Uncle Jack's sake. And Mom's.

"I'll wait for you at your locker," she said before hanging up.

"Good-bye," I said, beeping the phone off.

"That was an early morning phone call," Carrie taunted, grinning at me.

"Must be mighty important," I muttered under my breath.

♥ ♥ ♥

I took my time getting off the bus and walking up the steps to the school. It was nearly time for the first-period bell when I arrived at my locker.

A yellow Post-it was stuck to my locker. I HAVE TO TALK TO YOU! it read. Signed, Paula Miller.

Mission accomplished, I thought as I peeled it off and crumpled it into my pocket.

Somehow I managed to avoid Paula all day. And I didn't have to see her after school because she and the other church kids had gotten permission to leave class early for the Denver concert—during sixth period.

Before Jared left math class, he whispered, "I'll call you tomorrow, Holly-Heart." I could see Billy Hill and a bunch of kids waiting for him in the hallway. My heart sank. I could've been out there with Jared. If only . . .

"There will be no assignment for the weekend," the math teacher announced as the classroom door closed, shutting out the view to the hall.

No assignment, big deal. A small trade-off for being left behind.

Deserted and alone, I plodded off to my locker. Feeling low enough to crawl through the cracks at the base of my locker, I leaned against the door. Something poked into my forehead. I looked up. It was a note.

I pulled hard, finally retrieving it from its

hiding place. Unfolding it, I discovered Andie's message in the form of a note.

> *Dear Holly,*
>
> *Since you won't talk to me on the phone, I'm telling you straight. I had nothing to do with stealing your clothes on your birthday. It was Christiana's idea. I didn't even know about it till after school.*
>
> *I don't blame you for being mad. I would be, too. Wish you were coming tonight!*
>
> *Your friend,*
> *Andie*

I folded the note, feeling gloomy. Instead of riding the bus, I walked home in the freezing cold. The brisk air might clear out the cobwebs in my brain and the disappointment in my heart.

Jared was on his way to Denver without me. Tears sprang up in my eyes. Quickly, I wiped them away with my gloved hand. The wind chill was cold enough to freeze miniature icicles on my face. Another bus stop was two blocks ahead, but I chose to pass it up. Determined, I pushed my way through the ice and snow.

The first thing I did when I arrived home was to gather up my dirty clothes. It had been days since I'd done my laundry, and the hamper was swollen and overflowing. Besides, I owed someone a clean pair of jeans and a sweater. The cat killer.

Sorting through the white and colored clothes, I remembered the crazy dream I'd had. I could still see the images of designer labels and my clothes flying out of Andie's hands, plastering themselves against me, cold and unfriendly.

I sat down in the middle of the floor, hills of laundry piled on either side of me like mountains closing in, smothering me. Christiana and her scheme to steal Andie, Paula driving me nuts, and poor homeless Goofey . . .

Goofey. What was I going to do about him? The clinic couldn't keep him any longer; I'd inquired about it. Even if they could, I was broke. I couldn't bear to think of losing my sweet cat. Tears rolled down my cheeks. What if nobody wanted him? What if he had to be put to sleep?

I brushed away my tears. Lost in self-pity, I gathered up the whites and carried them down to the laundry just off the family room. Stan and the rest of the kids were playing a computer game. I sneaked past them unnoticed.

Back upstairs, I rummaged through all my jean pockets, cleaning out junk. My fingers found old tissues, loose change, and a tube of lip gloss. In the last pair, I discovered a piece of blue stationery with golden flecks, folded in two.

I studied it. The paper wasn't familiar, so I held up the jeans. They were Paula's. *This must belong to her,* I thought, setting it aside, debating what to do with it.

My curiosity won out. Slowly, I unfolded the paper.

> *Dearest Grandma:*
>
> *In response to your last letter, I have made no progress recruiting friends. Kayla seems satisfied with her one and only best friend—me.*
>
> *Being nice to Holly Meredith just isn't working. She has only one thing on her mind. That's Andie and the foreign exchange student, Christiana.*
>
> *Ever since we moved here, Holly has been upset with me. It was my fault, because I had a wild crush on her boyfriend, Jared Wilkins. But even when all that changed, it didn't seem to matter to Holly. She won't give me a chance and it hurts.*
>
> *Lately I've done everything imaginable to be nice to her, Grandma, hoping she'll change her mind. But she's not interested in me as a friend, and I'm so lonely sometimes I cry.*

I could read no further. Paula felt left out because of *me.* My unkind words, snide remarks . . . all of it bored into my soul.

The letter shook in my hand as the realization of who I was and what I'd done pierced through me. I was treating Paula exactly the way Andie had treated me. Ignoring her, rejecting her . . .

Carrying the letter to my window seat, I knelt down on the floor as tears streamed down my face. I didn't want to read the rest of her letter. Paula Miller had painted a deft description of Holly Meredith. Pathetic as I was.

16

I confessed my sins to God in prayer, then got up and recorded the event in my journal. I titled my entry and began to list the things I intended to change about myself.

MY "MOMENT OF TRUTH" LIST

I resolve to do the following:

___ 1. Make friends with many different girls.

___ 2. Say only good things about others, even behind their backs.

___ 3. Forgive Christiana for taking my clothes—and my best friend.

___ 4. Invite Andie, Christiana, and Paula to go skiing.

___ 5. Trust God for Goofey's future.

___ 6. Forget the idea of a number one best friend.

___ 7. Practice Matthew 5:44 every day of my life!

That done, I felt like Ebenezer Scrooge in the scene where he flings wide his window on Christmas Day. If only my friends were in town, I might hire a Goodyear blimp to broadcast my news. HOLLY MEREDITH COMES TO HER SENSES it might say. Or, A FABULOUS COLORADO WELCOME TO CHRISTIANA DERTNIG.

I floated downstairs on a cloud of transformation, greeting and hugging my family, including Carrie, who gave me a wide-eyed, cynical reception.

"How can I help you with supper?" I asked Mom.

"You may set the table," she said, pulling out the utensil drawer.

My initial thought was to remind Mom that it was Phil's chore, but I squelched it.

At supper I made sweet alien faces at Mark.

"Stop it," he said. "That's *my* thing." But by the grin on his face, I knew he loved it.

I addressed each member of the family with endearing terms. "Precious Phil, please pass the salad," I said without smirking.

"Knock it off, fish lips," he said.

But that didn't discourage me. "Stephie, sweets, pass the salt."

"Call me Stephie-Heart," she teased.

Uncle Jack had to interrupt my flow of

flowery expressions to announce the expansion of his business. "It's going to be big, and I mean *big*." He held up his water glass, proposing a toast.

Mom clinked her glass against his, beaming as she gazed at him. "And . . . it's a sure thing. We are definitely going skiing next weekend."

Phil and Mark cheered, Carrie and Stephie squealed, and Stan and I tipped our John Wayne "hats" at each other.

That night, after I read my devotional, I recommitted Goofey to God for safekeeping. "Please don't let him see my tears tomorrow when I go for the final visit," I prayed. "That's all I ask. Amen."

Settling down in my canopy bed, I fell asleep, clean as a kitten after a bubble bath.

♥   ♥   ♥

The next morning I awakened to Mom's lovely singing. She sounded as happy as I felt. I looked at the clock. Ten o'clock. I'd overslept!

Bouncing out of bed, I raced downstairs in my pajamas, first hugging Mom and Uncle Jack, then running upstairs to kiss Carrie and Stephie.

"Lay off," Carrie said, pushing me away.

Stephie hugged me back. "What's with Carrie?" she asked.

"Beats me, but maybe we can sweeten her up," I said, skipping to the bathroom to find some spray cologne.

"Leave me alone," Carrie hollered as I sprayed the air around her.

Just then, the doorbell rang. I dashed to my room, grabbing my bathrobe. Scrambling to the front door, I looked through the peephole.

It was Andie.

I looked closer and saw Christiana beside her. My heart thumped. A feeling of overwhelming delight filled me as I flung the door wide.

Andie studied me cautiously. Noting my smile, she broke into a mighty grin. "Happy belated birthday, Holly," she said.

"Come in, both of you," I said.

"We have a present for you," Andie said. She pointed at the white wicker basket she held. "It's not a joint present like last time. It's just, well . . . we worked out a little surprise."

Christiana seemed nervous. When I turned to her, she said, "I'm sorry about the birthday suit joke, Holly. It was a really mean thing to do."

Then she flashed a rueful grin at Andie. "I've learned a hard lesson, thanks to Andie," she admitted. "She hid our science project from me for twenty-four hours. Practical jokes are . . . well, simply not very practical." She extended her hand. "Sorry about taking your clothes. Friends?"

I hesitated a second. Had she given up her hand-zinging days, too? Then I shook her hand. "Friends," I agreed.

"Okay, Holly," Andie said. "Sit down." She led me to the rocking chair. "It's time for your present."

Bending over, Andie picked up the basket. It was decorated with a pink ribbon, my favorite color. She placed it on my lap.

I accepted the heavy basket, wondering what on earth she was up to now. "Thanks." I held the basket firmly. What could it be?

I felt Andie's eyes on me as I slowly opened the lid. There was something crocheted inside. It looked like one of Paula's creations.

But wait! Something moved beneath the mound of creamy-white yarn. A little pink nose nuzzled through a hole in the crocheted coverlet.

It was my cat, Goofey.

Tears clouded my eyes. "Oh, hello, baby," I whispered. I looked at Andie, amazed. "You brought him so I could say good-bye?"

Andie chuckled as Christiana pulled another present from her pocket. By now, Stephie and Carrie had wandered into the living room. They were making over Goofey like crazy. Thank goodness Mom was still upstairs.

"You're going to need this today," Christiana said.

"But—"

"Try opening it before you say anything," Andie said in her silliest voice.

"Here, hold my baby." I handed Goofey over to her so I could open the package.

Inside the wrapping paper was a bottle marked AllerCat. I held it up. "What's this?"

Andie looked like she was ready to pop. But it was Christiana who responded. "If you apply this liquid to Goofey's skin as the directions recommend, your stepdad should have complete relief from his allergy."

"Really?" I looked at Andie. "Are you sure?"

Andie nodded. "Christiana told me about it. I tried and tried to call you and tell you, but, well, let's just forget about that."

Christiana stroked Goofey's neck.

"It's a miracle." I hugged them both. "Thanks for being my friends."

My birthday wish had come true after all.

"Mom," I called. "Come quick!"

The living room was already crammed with Stan, Phil, and Mark who had wandered in, drawn by the commotion. Uncle Jack came wearing grubby jeans and a big grin. Carrie and

Stephie took turns holding, stroking, and whispering to Goofey. And then Mom arrived, flying through the middle of them like Mary Poppins.

"Mom, this is so fabulous," I said. "Goofey's back home to stay." Before she could launch a protest, I quickly read out loud the directions on the back of the bottle.

"Well, why didn't *we* think of this?" Mom said cheerfully.

That's when I did it. I asked Andie and Christiana to come skiing with us the following weekend.

"Let's do," Christiana said.

"Love to," Andie replied, zipping her jacket.

"Thanks for the kitty surprise," I said, addressing both Andie and Christiana as they headed for the door. "It's the perfect gift." And I meant it.

I took Goofey from Stephie and followed my friends to the front porch. "How was the concert?" I asked.

"Mandee is amazing in person," Andie said.

"She really is," Christiana said. "I bought all her CDs."

"And that's not all," Andie said, grinning. "Christiana wants to know more about God."

"Hey, that's fabulous," I said, sorry I hadn't treated her better all along. I gave her another hug.

"I have a lot to learn," Christiana said. "But Andie has two Bibles."

Andie nodded. "And she's coming to church with us tomorrow."

"Cool. I'll see you there," I said as they turned to leave. Then I asked, "Did Paula have a good time last night?" I actually held my breath, waiting for an answer.

"I think so, why?" Andie asked.

"It's a long story," I said as they waved. "I'll tell you sometime."

Christiana floated down the front porch steps, turning to wave again several more times.

"Come again," I called to them.

Then, snuggling Goofey close, I went inside. "It's time to give you a bath in something very special." I reached for the bottle of AllerCat. "This will keep Mom and Uncle Jack happy. Besides that, you're going to have a very special visitor today."

Carrie and Stephie followed me to the bathroom. "Who's coming over?" Carrie asked.

I answered in a mysterious voice. "I'll never tell."

"But you have to," Stephie said, pulling my arm.

After applying AllerCat as the instructions directed, I wrapped the pink bow around Goofey's neck.

Then I marched to the phone in the hallway and dialed.

"Paula?" I said when she answered. It wasn't hard to imagine her smile. And for the first time, I didn't immediately think of a toothpaste commercial.

"This is your friend Holly, and there's someone here who misses you." I held Goofey up to the phone. He meowed twice on cue. Just the way a perfectly pampered and well-mannered pet should.

♥   ♥   ♥

Don't miss HOLLY'S HEART #7,
Good-Bye, Dressel Hills
Available November 2002!

Holly's stepfather has gotten a new job—in Denver! Holly has only two weeks to say good-bye to her friends in Dressel Hills. Will she keep a long-distance relationship with Jared? A day of packing leaves Holly devastated after uncovering the truth about her parents' divorce.

About the Author

Beverly Lewis has developed friendships with "kids" of all ages—first graders she meets in school visits, teens who email her for advice, and senior adults who buy her books for their grandkids, as well as novels for themselves.

"Not many friends are loyal all the time," says Beverly, "but Jesus Christ is the ultimate best friend. Proverbs 18:24 says He 'sticks closer than a brother.' Now that's my kind of friend!"

Beverly loves getting mail from her reader friends. If you want to write, her address options are as follows:

Email address: *www.BeverlyLewis.com*
Or . . . snail mail: Beverly Lewis
    Bethany House Publishers
    11400 Hampshire Avenue South
    Bloomington, MN 55438

Also by Beverly Lewis

PICTURE BOOKS

Cows in the House   Annika's Secret Wish
Just Like Mama

THE CUL-DE-SAC KIDS
Children's Fiction

The Double Dabble Surprise   Tarantula Toes
The Chicken Pox Panic   Green Gravy
The Crazy Christmas Angel Mystery   Backyard Bandit Mystery
No Grown-ups Allowed   Tree House Trouble
Frog Power   The Creepy Sleep-Over
The Mystery of Case D. Luc   The Great TV Turn-Off
The Stinky Sneakers Mystery   Piggy Party
Pickle Pizza   The Granny Game
Mailbox Mania   Mystery Mutt
The Mudhole Mystery   Big Bad Beans
Fiddlesticks   The Upside-Down Day
The Crabby Cat Caper   The Midnight Mystery

ABRAM'S DAUGHTERS
Adult Fiction

The Covenant

THE HERITAGE OF LANCASTER COUNTY
Adult Fiction

The Shunning   The Confession
The Reckoning

OTHER ADULT FICTION

The Postcard

The Crossroad

October Song

The Redemption of Sarah Cain

Sanctuary*

The Sunroom

www.BeverlyLewis.com

*with David Lewis

PUT YOUR LIFE
ON THE RIGHT PATH

1. Get God
2. Wise Up
3. Cross Train
4. Pray Hard
5. See Jesus
6. Stick Tight
7. Get Smart
8. Bust Loose

Bible Studies Written Just for You!

Kevin Johnson's EARLY TEEN DISCIPLESHIP series is unique
in that it's designed for kids your age, pointing you toward
a vital, heart-to-heart, sold-out relationship with God. Each
book contains twenty-five topical studies that will help you
understand and live your faith.

BETHANYHOUSE 11400 Hampshire Ave S. Minneapolis, MN 55438
(800) 328-6109 www.bethanyhouse.com